# Whatever After

## BAD HAIR DAY

# Whatever After

## BAD HAIR DAY

### SARAH MLYNOWSKI

Scholastic Inc.

*for my editor, aimee friedman —*
*you are a true gem.*

This book was originally published in hardcover by Scholastic Press in 2014.

ISBN 978-0-545-62729-0

12 11 10 9 8 7 6 5 4 3 2 1    15 16 17 18 19 20/0

Printed in the U.S.A.    40
This edition first printing, April 2015

# \* chapter one \*

## Today Is Not a Good Day

I slump into a chair at the kitchen table.

"So what's wrong?" my little brother, Jonah, asks.

It's five o'clock, and the almost setting sun streams through the windows, making me shield my eyes. "I don't want to talk about it," I mutter. When my dad picked us up from school, I told him the same thing. My best friends, Robin and Frankie, have already called twice since I got home to see how I'm feeling, but I don't want to talk to them about it, either.

Jonah hunts through the cupboard and takes out a bag of chips. "You sure? You look upset."

I *am* upset. Maybe I DO want to talk about it? I swallow the lump in my throat. "I didn't win the class spelling bee," I finally admit.

You might be wondering: Abby, why are you so upset you didn't win the spelling bee? Did you expect to win the spelling bee?

My answer: Yes! I did expect to win the spelling bee! I ALWAYS win the spelling bee.

Case in point:

In third grade I won the spelling bee.

In fourth grade I won the spelling bee.

But what happened in fifth grade? Did I win the spelling bee? NO. I did not.

In fifth grade, today, I LOST THE SPELLING BEE.

"Did you come in second?" Jonah asks. He takes a bottle of ketchup out of the fridge, sits down in the seat across from me, and squirts the ketchup directly onto a chip.

"No."

"Did you come in third?"

"No," I snap.

He scrunches his eyebrows. "Fourth?"

I bite the inside of my cheek.

"Fifth?"

I explode. "Ninth! Okay? I came in ninth!"

Jonah's eyes widen. A ketchup-soaked chip falls out of his hand onto the table.

"I know!" I cry. "I'm just as shocked as you are!"

I can't stop the scene at school from replaying in my head. It was my turn again. I was standing confidently among the remaining eight students at the front of the room. I gave the kids who'd already been eliminated my most compassionate smile. I waited for Ms. Masserman to tell me my word. . . .

"Maybe you're just not a good speller," Jonah says, interrupting my playback. He pops another chip into his mouth.

"I am, too, a good speller!" I say, my face flushing.

"Maybe you used to be a good speller compared to the kids in your *old* class," Jonah explains. "But you're not a good speller compared to the kids in your new class. Or maybe the words just got harder."

I nod twice. "They *did* get harder."

"What word did you mess up?" he asks.

My chest tightens. *"Cinnamon."*

Suddenly, I'm right back there in the classroom, remembering how it felt to have everyone's eyes on me.

"C-I-N-A-M-M-I-N," I'd spelled out with assurance. I waited for my teacher's smile. Or maybe a thumbs-up. Or perhaps applause?

"I'm sorry, Abby," Ms. Masserman said, pinching her lips as if she'd just tasted something sour. Like vinegar. Definitely not cinnamon. "That's incorrect."

Huh? What?

"The correct spelling for cinnamon is C-I-N-*N*-A-*M-O*-N," she said. "Abby, you're out. Penny, your turn again."

My body froze. My neck. My back. My feet. "But . . ." My voice trailed off.

"Yes?" Ms. Masserman asked.

"Can I try again?" I whispered.

"Sorry, Abby. One strike per student."

My throat closed up. Tears pricked my eyes. I would not cry in school. I WOULD. NOT. CRY. IN. SCHOOL.

I cried in school.

It was horrible.

I asked to go to the restroom as the tears dripped down my cheeks.

"Crybaby," Penny muttered as I left.

A few of the kids laughed. Not Robin and Frankie, obviously. I heard Robin ask if she could be excused, too, but Ms. Masserman said no.

After ten minutes of sulking in the bathroom, I pulled myself together and returned to class. I avoided all eye contact.

Now, sitting in the kitchen with Jonah, I shudder with embarrassment at the memory.

I put my head on the kitchen table and groan.

"Did everyone get such hard words?" Jonah asks.

"Well, Frankie got "quandary," which I can totally spell even though it's hard. I *know* I'm the best speller in the class."

Jonah rolls his eyes. "Okay, Miss Conceited."

I cringe. I'll admit that sounded a little obnoxious. "I guess what I mean is I *thought* I was the best speller in the class. . . ."

I trail off. Am I not as smart as I think I am? Maybe I'm not smart at all. But if I'm not smart . . . what am I?

Ms. Masserman gave me a certificate that says THIS IS TO CERTIFY THAT ABBY PARTICIPATED IN OUR CLASS SPELLING BEE.

Did she think I would hang that up in my room? When my bulletin board already has two spelling bee certificates that both say CHAMPION on them? No way.

I feel the tears behind my eyelids again, and I blink. There. That's better. "I don't want to talk about the stupid spelling bee anymore," I say to Jonah. "Tell me about your day."

My brother grins. "I had a great day."

"Oh yeah? What happened to make it so great?" I snag one of his potato chips and pop it into my mouth.

"Two things. One, I got new cleats."

"Huh?"

"Dad got me new cleats for soccer. They're in the living room. They are really cool."

Hmm. "You get new soccer shoes and I get ninth place in a spelling bee?"

He nods.

"Wanna trade?" I half smile.

He munches another chip. "You don't play soccer. And I don't know how to spell 'cinnamon' or 'quandary,' either. I don't even know what a quandary is. Is it a place to put ducks?"

"It means a sticky situation," I say. "What's the second great thing?"

"I learned an awesome new song. Wanna hear?"

"Sure," I say.

He clears his throat: *"I know a song that gets on everybody's nerves, everybody's nerves, everybody's nerves. I know a song that gets on everybody's nerves, and this is how it goes: I know a song that gets on everybody's nerves, everybody's nerves, everybody's nerves —"*

"All right, that's enough," I say.

*"I know a song that gets on everybody's nerves, everybody's nerves, everybody's nerves —"*

"I'm going to do my homework," I say, standing up. "This isn't helping my mood." It feels like there's something pointy pushing down on my chest. Soccer cleats, maybe.

I drag my feet all the way up the stairs to my bedroom. I can hear my dad on the phone down in the basement. My mom is still at her office. They're both lawyers and they work a lot.

Even when I close my bedroom door, I can still hear Jonah singing.

Our new puppy, Prince, is playing with an old tennis ball on my carpet. He jumps up when he sees me. He nuzzles his little, dark brown nose against my foot. Then he rubs his light brown cheek against my other foot and looks up at me with his big, chocolate eyes.

"Hi, cutie," I say, crouching down and scratching behind his floppy ears. "You still love me even though I can't spell, right?"

Instead of answering, he licks my face. Or maybe that's his way of answering.

Yup, Prince does still love me. And I love him. He's sweet and bouncy and very, very smart. Last week I'm pretty sure he folded my sweater and put it away in my drawer.

Okay, that was probably my mom. But still. We've only had him a few weeks and he already knows how to "sit," "stay," "come here," and that he should wait until he's outside to go to the bathroom. I trained him myself. Okay, my mom did that, too, but I definitely helped.

Prince followed us back from the last fairy tale Jonah and I visited. We didn't mean to take him with us, but now he's ours. Our parents said we could keep him if his owner didn't come forward. Of course no owner came forward. His original owner lives in a kingdom on the other side of our magic mirror.

Did I mention that we have a magic mirror in our basement? Well, we do. If we knock on the mirror at midnight, it takes Jonah and me into fairy tales. So far, we've visited Snow White, Cinderella, the Little Mermaid, and Sleeping Beauty. We go through the mirror, we change the stories, and then we come home. Of course, we don't *mean* to change the stories. Well, usually we don't. But they all end up changed.

You probably think I'm making that up. But I'm not. I'm being one hundred percent honest!

I scoot over to the jewelry box my nana got me a few years ago. The box features all the famous fairy tale characters. Most of them used to be in normal, expected poses. You know — the Little Mermaid with her tail. Snow White with her apple. Now all the stories we've been to have new pictures to go with their new endings. Their new *happy* endings.

I plop facedown on my bedspread. At least *they're* happy.

I hear Jonah thump his way up the stairs and into his room. He's *still* singing. "*. . . a song that gets on everybody's nerves, everybody's —*"

I prop myself up on one elbow. "Jonah!" I shout. "Enough already! You've officially gotten on my nerves! Now get off them!"

Silence. Two seconds later, my door opens.

Prince yips happily.

"Don't you knock?" I murmur, my face planted in my bed-spread again.

"Okay, grumpy-head, I know just what will cheer you up," I hear Jonah say.

"Is it you not singing that annoying song?"

"No! We should go through the mirror tonight," he chirps.

I flip over and stare at my ceiling. "Don't feel like it," I grumble.

"That's exactly why we have to do it. You're sad. Fairy tale land will make you un-sad. It's fun."

"Sometimes it's fun; sometimes we get into all kinds of trouble," I argue. "Like almost drowning or being turned into mice. And anyway, I don't want to have fun. I want to sit in my room and be miserable. I'm not going."

Jonah plugs his fingers into his ears. "I can't hear you, I can't hear you! I'll come get you at midnight!"

"No, Jonah —" I start, but he's already backed out of the room.

# * chapter two *

## SHHHHHHH

C ome on, Abby, let's go!"

I open my eyes. My brother is standing over me. I groan, seeing that my clock says 11:55 P.M.

"Jonah, no!" I snap. "I told you I don't want to go through the mirror tonight!"

"Come on," he says. "It'll be an adventure!"

My brother loves adventure. He's the kind of kid who goes rock climbing. For *fun*. And not because someone is, say, chasing him up a mountain. He actually takes a rock-climbing class every weekend.

Sometimes I love adventure, too. But not tonight. "If you want an adventure so badly, go yourself," I say.

"We always go together," he says with a pout.

True. We *do* always go together. Which is probably for the best. Who knows what would happen to Jonah if I weren't there to help him? He'd probably have been eaten by a crocodile by now. Still . . .

"I'm not coming," I say.

He puts his hands on his hips. "Fine. I'll go by myself."

I snort-laugh. "You will not."

"Will too!" He spins on his heel and scurries toward the door.

Yeah, whatever. He's not *really* going to go without me.

"Later," Jonah says, and closes my door on his way out.

He's just calling my bluff.

I put my head back down on my pillow and force my eyes closed.

He wouldn't *really* go by himself. Would he? My heart speeds up. What if something bad happens to him? What if he gets attacked by another crocodile? Or a witch? Or a wolf? Anything is possible in fairy tale land!

I sit up in bed. I can't let him go by himself — it's my job as big sister to protect him.

I swiftly change into jeans and an orange hoodie, grab my watch, lace up my sneakers, and throw open my door.

Jonah is standing in the hallway just outside my room, with a huge smile. "Sucker."

I roll my eyes. "I should have known. I'm going back to bed."

"You are not!" Jonah exclaims. "You're already dressed."

He has a point. Besides, it *is* pretty exciting to go through the mirror.

"Shhh! All right, all right, let's go," I whisper. We can't wake our parents. According to one of the fairies we met in our travels, we're supposed to keep the whole magic mirror thing to ourselves. But keeping a magic mirror secret is harder than it looks. Last trip, we almost got busted.

"Jonah," I whisper, glancing down at my brother's feet. "You're not wearing shoes. And go put on a hoodie. What if we end up in *The Snow Queen*? It's cold there!"

"Oops," he says. "Be right back. I'll meet you in the basement."

"Don't wake up Prince!" I order. Prince sleeps on a doggie bed in Jonah's room.

I sigh as I open the basement door and climb down the steps.

I can't believe I'm really doing this. I stop and look at the mirror. It's attached to the wall with heavy bolts. It has a stone frame that's engraved with small fairies with wings and wands.

Maybe Maryrose won't even let us in. Usually, all I have to do to get in is knock on the mirror three times. But not always. Sometimes we knock and knock and knock and Maryrose doesn't answer. Sometimes we need to be wearing something special, like a bathing suit or flag-colored pajamas, which will help us when we're in the story. The problem is that we never know *what* we need to be wearing since we never know what story we're going to before we get there.

Maryrose is the fairy who lives inside our mirror. At least we think she lives inside it. Maybe she just visits it when we knock on it. We're not one hundred percent sure.

I hear my brother clomping down the basement stairs.

He's SO loud. Is he TRYING to wake up our parents and get us in trouble?

I scowl at the mirror. My reflection scowls back.

Besides the scowl, I look just like I always do. Same curly brown hair. Same big green eyes. Same freckles. In the mirror's surface, I watch Jonah hurry toward me. Like me, he's wearing jeans. He picked a yellow hoodie. Mine is orange. We are very bright. Hopefully, we won't have to do much hiding in tonight's fairy tale. Unless we're hiding in a fruit salad.

"Ready?" I say. "Let's get this over with."

I lift my hand up to knock, grateful that I remembered to put on my watch. The thing about my watch is that no matter what day or time it is in the fairy tale, my watch always tells me the time at home. It is extremely helpful to know what time it is back home so Jonah and I know how long we have until our parents wake up. We try to be home *before* our parents wake up, which is at seven in the morning.

I knock. Once. Twice. Three times. The reflection doesn't budge.

"Can I go back to bed now?" I ask, crossing my arms.

"Let me try," Jonah says. He knocks once. Firmly. Loudly.

*Hissss.*

"It's working!" Jonah cries.

Hooray?

He knocks the second time. A purple glow spreads across the room.

Last knock . . .

The reflection in the mirror begins to swirl.

"Hooray!" Jonah cheers.

I feel the familiar pull. It's like someone is gently tugging on my hair. I shrug. "All right. I guess we're going."

Suddenly, I hear: *"Ruff! Ruff, ruff, ruff!"*

I spin around to see Prince leaping down the stairs toward the mirror.

"Jonah!" I cry, bending down and trying to stop Prince from jumping into the mirror. "You woke up Prince! And you left the basement door open!"

Jonah grimaces. "Oops. But can't Prince come, too? He'll help. He'll love it."

"No, he can't come," I snap. "What if we lose him? His leash is upstairs."

Jonah frowns. "Oh, right."

"Sit, Prince, sit," I order.

Instead of sitting, Prince jumps up on my legs.

*"Ruff, ruff, ruff!"*

"Stay, Prince, stay! Sit, Prince, sit!"

Prince does not sit. Prince does not stay. Prince tries to squirm around me.

"If you stay I'll give you a million pumpkin seeds when we get back," I promise. Prince loves pumpkin seeds. Also peanut butter.

The gentle pull has turned into a stronger pull. It now feels as though I'm standing in front of a vacuum cleaner set on HIGH. My sneakers grind against the floor as the mirror pulls me toward it. "Go back upstairs, Prince. Please? Stop barking!" I say. But Prince's barks are getting louder. "Shhh! Prince! You have to be quiet! You'll wake up Mom and Dad!" Why isn't he listening? I swear, he used to listen to me.

"Let's just take him," Jonah says. "C'mon!"

"It's not a good idea," I say. "It is very irresponsible! We don't even have his doggie poop bags!"

*"Ruff, ruff, ruff, RUFF!"*

I don't think I can hold myself back anymore. My body is a magnet, and the mirror is a fridge. I try one last time. "I'll give you an entire jar of peanut butter if you go back upstairs, Prince!"

With a final loud bark, Prince leaps between my feet, and dives paws-first into the mirror.

"Wait!" I yell. I grab my brother's hand and we follow Prince inside.

# * chapter three *

## Now Where Are We?

We land with a thump.

Ouch.

I'm facedown on my stomach, my chin in the mud, my wrist under my head. The ground is hard and grassy. It's quiet. I see lots of tree trunks and tree roots. Why is my head lower than my feet? Am I on a slant? Yes, I think I am! Actually, I think I'm on a hill. I try to stand up, but the angle I'm at makes it too hard, since I'm going against gravity.

Jonah's feet are right beside me. He's lying on his back.

"So are you feeling cheered up?" Jonah asks me.

"No," I say. "My chin hurts. Help me up?"

Prince nuzzles his nose into my ear and then licks it.

"Hello there," I say.

Prince wags his tail.

"Did you have to bark so loudly before you left?" I ask him. If Mom and Dad woke up to an empty house in the middle of the night, we'd be in BIG trouble. As if today could get any worse.

Jonah manages to get up, and then he helps me stand. I get to my feet unsteadily, feeling a little dizzy.

I wipe the dirt off my jeans and glance at all the trees. Now that I'm vertical, I can see green leaves and some patches of blue sky. It smells like pine. We're on a hill in a forest.

"Where do you think we are?" Jonah asks, looking around.

Good question. "What fairy tale is in a forest?" I wonder out loud.

Jonah's eyes widen. "The one with the wolf!"

"*Little Red Riding Hood*?"

"Yes!" He smiles gleefully. "That would be so much fun!"

I shiver. "Bumping into a wolf that might try to eat us does not sound fun to me AT ALL."

My brother loves the scary parts of the fairy tales. They're the only parts he remembers. Like wolves who eat children and stepsisters who cut off their toes. Yes, that seriously happened in the original *Cinderella*. Ouch.

We know a lot of the originals because our nana used to read them to us all the time when we lived near her. She's a literature professor at a college in Chicago. Also, ever since I first fell into the mirror, I reread a lot of the stories, of course.

But maybe Jonah is right. Maybe we *are* in *Little Red Riding Hood*.

"Little Red Riding Hood?" I call out. "Are you there? Are you going to visit your grandma's house?"

I hear a noise coming from my left.

Prince turns toward it and barks.

"Did you hear that?" I ask Jonah, grabbing his arm.

"No, I —" he starts to say, but I shush him with my hand, listening hard.

The noise isn't a wolf. It's singing! Yes! Someone is singing!

*"The leaf falling from a tree,*
*Beautiful but so lone-ly . . ."*

"I heard that, too!" Jonah squeals. "It sounds like music. Little Red Riding Hood is singing!"

"It might not be Little Red Riding Hood," I say. I try to move toward the voice. It's coming from below us. Is the person at the bottom of the hill? Or is someone in the ground? Is there a fairy tale about people who live in the ground?

I step around the tree and can make out a building in the distance.

A tower. At the bottom of the hill.

A beige stone tower with an open window at the top.

Jonah sees it, too. "Maybe we're back in *Sleeping Beauty*?" he offers.

"It's not the same tower as in *Sleeping Beauty*," I say. "It's a different color. And there's no palace nearby. And we're on a hill."

I look around again. We're kind of in the middle of nowhere. I think hard. Middle of nowhere . . . tower . . . singing . . .

*"Alone in the world with nobody there,*
*My only friend is my beautiful hair."*

. . . hair!

"We're in *Rapunzel*!" I cry. "Yes! Rapunzel sings! That's how the prince hears her!"

Prince the dog barks.

I lean down and scratch his head. "Not you, Prince. The other prince."

"Rapunzel? She's the one with the long hair, right?" Jonah asks.

"Yes. Really, *really* long hair."

"Did we see the movie?"

"We did, but the real story is *very* different from the movie," I explain, straightening up. "In the real story, Rapunzel isn't a secret princess. She's a regular girl who ends up marrying a prince —"

*"Ruff, ruff!"*

"I wish we had dog treats with us," Jonah says. He bends down to scratch Prince under the chin.

"We didn't exactly know he was coming, did we?" I point out.

"Maybe Rapunzel has peanut butter."

That would help. Also a leash.

I glance toward the tower and see a flash of dark hair in the window.

"I just saw her!" I exclaim, feeling a burst of excitement. At least I think it's her. For some reason, I thought Rapunzel was blond. Maybe I imagined that or remembered it from the movie.

"Cool!" Jonah says, standing on his toes to try to get a look.

"So, back to the story," I say, nudging him. "There was a nice, normal couple who were expecting a baby. But they lived next door to a witch. The witch's name was Frau Gothel —"

"Her first name was Frown?"

"No. Frau. 'Frau' means 'Mrs.' in German. The Grimm Brothers wrote the story."

"They write all the stories."

"A lot of them," I agree. "Anyway, Frown — I mean Frau — Gothel had a garden with all kinds of herbs and plants. And the pregnant woman was craving rapunzel. That's a kind of herb. It's green and leafy."

"Did Mom have cravings when she was pregnant with me?" Jonah asks.

"Probably," I say with a chuckle. "I wouldn't be surprised if she ate a ton of ketchup."

Jonah's eyes light up. "Hey! That's the first time you've laughed since you got home from school. I told you going through the mirror was a good idea!"

I stop smiling. "I'm still upset about the spelling bee."

"Just go on with the story," Jonah says, smiling playfully.

My brother isn't wrong — going through the mirror has definitely been a good distraction. But that doesn't mean I'm over my bad day at school. Trying to brush off the memory, I continue.

"The mother-to-be really wanted some rapunzel. In fact, she said she would *die* if she didn't get any. So the dad snuck into the witch's garden and stole some. Except" — I make a pretend drumroll in the air — "the witch caught him!"

"Oh, no!"

"Oh, yes. Frau Gothel said that she would only let the dad take the rapunzel *if* he gave her the baby when the baby was born."

Jonah's eyes bulge. "To keep?"

"Yes."

"I hope the dad told her no way."

"He didn't. He agreed. He was terrified his wife was really going to die without the herb. Maybe he hoped the witch would forget about the promise by the time the baby was born."

"Did she?"

"Nope. Frau Gothel took the baby and named her Rapunzel, after the herb. When Rapunzel was twelve, the witch brought her to a tower and locked her inside. There was no door or stairway — only a window."

Jonah glances over at the far-off tower. "It doesn't look like there's any way up. Maybe they rock climbed it."

"I doubt it. But the witch would come visit Rapunzel every day. She'd say, 'Rapunzel, Rapunzel, let down your hair.' And Rapunzel would let her hair down, and the witch would climb up."

Jonah shakes his head. "But why would she let the witch up?"

"Maybe she needed food. Or maybe she was lonely. Maybe she thought Frau Gothel was really her mother."

Jonah wrinkles his nose. "What kind of mother keeps her kid locked in a tower?"

"A very bad one. Anyway, one day, a prince —"

*"Ruff, ruff!"*

"— was passing by and he heard the singing." I stop talking for a second to see if Rapunzel is still singing. She is. Also, I think I hear chimes. And a drum? Is she playing instruments, too?

"Anyway," I continue, "he thought the girl in the tower had a very pretty voice. So he went back to the tower again and again, until one day he heard the witch tell the girl to let her hair down, and then he saw the witch climb up. He came back that night and said the same thing the witch had. And when Rapunzel let her hair down, the prince —"

*"Ruff, ruff!"*

I look down at Prince and realize he's staring expectantly at me. Oh! "Every time we say the word 'prince,' he thinks we're talking to him. I'm going to need to come up with a new name if I'm going to tell this story without getting a headache. Let's call the prince —"

*"Ruff, ruff!"*

"Pickles!" Jonah cries gleefully.

My brother is so weird. "Why?"

He bounces on his sneakers. "Why not? I like pickles! Don't you?"

"All right, all right. So when Rapunzel let her hair down, Pickles climbed up, and they fell in love. He secretly climbed up every night to see her. Except by accident one time Rapunzel told the witch that she was heavier than Pickles, and the witch figured it out. She was so mad, she cut off Rapunzel's hair and banished Rapunzel from the tower. Rapunzel had nowhere to go and wandered around the forest. That night, when Pickles showed up at the tower, Frau Gothel hung Rapunzel's braid out the window and pretended to be her. When Pickles climbed up, she told him that he would never see Rapunzel again. He jumped out the window and landed in thorns — and the thorns made him *blind*! He wandered around the forest for years until he finally heard a familiar voice singing, and he realized it was Rapunzel. She cried when she found him, and her tears spilled into his eyes and brought back his sight."

Jonah's jaw drops. "She had magic tears! How come?"

"Maybe because of the rapunzel her mother ate? I don't know. Anyway, Rapunzel and Pickles lived —"

"Happily ever after," Jonah finishes, nodding. "What happened to the witch?"

I shrug. "No idea."

He leans closer. "What happened to Rapunzel's parents?"

I shrug again. "Also no idea."

Jonah and I both glance at the tower. Rapunzel is still singing inside.

"What do we do now?" Jonah asks me.

"We should probably go home," I say with a sigh. "Rapunzel gets her happily-ever-after. We don't need to mess it up."

My brother's eyes widen. "You want to leave right away? You don't even want to meet Rapunzel?"

My heart leaps. Of course I *want* to meet her. Who wouldn't want to meet Rapunzel?

"Do you think we could meet her without messing anything up?" I wonder out loud. "We could just say hello and then leave? Although we'd still have to figure out how to get home . . ."

"Of course we can!" Jonah exclaims, ignoring my last sentence. "Let's go!" He starts running down the hill toward the tower.

I can't help it. I follow. I REALLY WANT TO MEET RAPUNZEL!

Also, running down hills is fun. *Wheeeeeeee!*

Prince scurries along behind us, yapping at my heels.

I'm having such a good time, I almost forget about the spelling bee disaster. *Almost.*

By the time we get to the base of the tower, the singing has stopped. I peer up at the window but don't see the flash of hair again. I hope it really *is* Rapunzel inside. It has to be, right?

Jonah and I examine the base of the tower. There are thorny bushes all around it. Yikes.

"There doesn't seem to be a door here," Jonah says.

"I know," I say.

"How do you want to do this?" Jonah asks. "Do you want to just yell hello and wait for her to poke her head out? Or . . ."

"Or what?" I ask. "What else can I do? She doesn't have a cell phone. I can't exactly call her."

"No, but you can go up," Jonah says with a grin.

"How?" I ask. "Do you see an elevator?"

"Abby!" He tugs at my arm. "Come on! Don't you want to climb up her hair?"

*Gasp.*

I didn't realize until he said it, but now that he did, I can't believe I didn't think of it myself. Yes, *yes*, YES! Of course I want to climb up her hair! I nod. I giggle. I nod again.

"I do," I whisper. "I really, really do."

Jonah waves his hands in the air. "Say the magic words, then."

What does he mean? "Pretty please?"

He laughs. "No! The Rapunzel ones!"

I slap my palm against my forehead. Of course! Then I clear my throat. Is this going to work? Only one way to find out.

"Rapunzel, Rapunzel," I say. "Let down your hair."

I wait. Nothing happens.

Jonah shakes his head. "I think you have to be louder than that. She's pretty high up."

He's right. I clear my throat again. "Rapunzel, Rapunzel!" I call out a little louder. "Let down your hair!"

He shakes his head again. "C'mon, Abby, louder than that!"

"RAPUNZEL, RAPUNZEL!" I yell, as if I'm playing red rover. "LET DOWN YOUR HAIR!"

And then, before I even know what's happening, a long, long dark braid is falling from the window. I jump out of the way at the last minute so it won't crush me.

But it wouldn't. It stops at my knees. A bright blue ribbon is tied at the very end of the braid.

I cannot believe it worked. I told Rapunzel to let down her hair and she did!

It's a beautiful braid, too. It has four thick sections, all woven expertly together. I would never be able to make a braid that perfect even if I spent all day on it. And I'm a pretty good hairdresser. I used to style and cut my dolls' hair all the time.

"What do we do?" I ask in disbelief.

Jonah rolls his eyes. "Come on, Abby. We climb it!"

# ✳ chapter four ✳

## Up, Up, and Away

I take a deep breath. I reach out to put my hands around the braid.

Rapunzel's hair feels silky. Like Mom's hair after she blow-dries it straight.

Behind us, Prince barks again.

"Sit, Prince, sit!" I say. "Wait for us right here."

He keeps barking and begins chasing his tail.

"What are we going to do with him?" I ask. "We can't just leave him here. What if he runs away?"

"I'll carry him," Jonah says. "Don't worry. I'm super good at it. I bet I can do this with one hand."

Should I be nervous that my seven-year-old brother is planning to climb a tower with one hand?

Probably.

Do I have a choice?

No.

I hold on securely to the braid and then try to step up the wall. The braid sways, and I trip. "Um, I don't think this is going to work," I tell Jonah.

"Can you put your feet into the spaces of the braid like a ladder?" Jonah suggests.

"Um . . ." I try. The spaces are too small. The tips of my feet don't fit. I land back down on the ground. Argh! I came all the way here and I won't even be able to climb Rapunzel's braid. This is the worst day ever. I should have stayed in bed!

"I have another idea," Jonah says.

"Does this idea involve an escalator?"

"Try climbing it like you would a rope in gym class."

Oh! I've done that! I haven't done it *well*, but I've done it. I grab the braid again.

"Hold on to the rope — I mean hair — with your hands," Jonah instructs patiently, "and also squeeze it between your feet."

I do as I'm told. The tower is about four stories high. This is going to take a while.

"Good. Now grab a little higher on the rope with your hands."

I grab higher. Just a little higher, but still higher.

"Now lift up your legs a little higher."

I do it.

"There you go!" Jonah shouts. "You're climbing!"

I am! Awesome!

"You can also wrap the rope around the bottom of your foot," Jonah advises. "That's harder, though. It's advanced. I saw a seventh grader doing it. I'm going to try it."

More advanced? Is he kidding me?

The hair is so smooth, it's slippery. My heart pounds as I grip the braid extra hard so I won't fall. I have to squeeze it. My knuckles are turning white. I carefully pull myself up, inch by inch. My arms hurt, but I keep going. Higher and higher and higher. It's a tiny bit scary, but also sort of fun. I'm doing it, I'm doing it! The wind is whistling in my ears! Wheee! I'm climbing Rapunzel's hair!

When I finally reach the top, I pull myself onto the ledge of the glassless window.

A teenage girl wearing a loose blue dress is sitting in a wooden chair with her back to me. Her beautiful, dark brown hair is pulled back in a braid that trails all the way down her back, over the chair, and out the window.

I stay seated on the ledge and clear my throat. "Excuse me? Rapunzel? Your name is Rapunzel, right?"

The girl spins around and leaps out of her chair. Her mouth drops open in shock. "You're not Frau Gothel!" she cries. She hugs her braid to her chest. She looks completely terrified. As if she just saw a ghost.

"I'm sorry for scaring you!" I say. "I'm Abby!"

"Don't come any closer!" Her left arm shoots out as though she's trying to protect herself. Or maybe she's trying to protect her hair.

"I'm harmless!" I tell her. "Don't be afraid! I'm only ten! And . . . I heard you singing," I add quickly. "And you were really good. I wanted to say hello!"

She blushes. "You did? That's so embarrassing! I never would have sung if I knew someone was listening."

"Well, you have a great voice," I tell her. "And I loved your song."

She blushes more deeply. "My songs are silly. A way to pass the time."

"I didn't think your song was silly. I thought it was fun. I love your hair, too," I say. "I can't believe how strong it is."

Her shoulders relax. "Frau Gothel gets me all kinds of fancy shampoos and conditioners and oil treatments to use. I take good care of it." She pats her braid lovingly. Then she bites her lower lip. "She would not be happy that you are here. I'm not supposed to have visitors."

"We really wanted to meet you," I say.

She glances around anxiously and coils her braid around her arm so that it no longer hangs out the window. "We? Who's we? Is there someone else here?"

"My brother is still on the ground," I explain. "He's only seven. Oh! And Prince. Not the real prince. Our dog, Prince. He's only a puppy. He's well trained, though. Kind of." I cough. "Can they come up, too?"

"I don't know," she says, blinking repeatedly. "I'm *really* not supposed to let anyone besides Frau up."

"We'll be fast," I promise. "In and out. We just want to say hi and then we'll go. It'll be like we were never here."

Rapunzel hesitates. "Well . . . all right. It *is* nice to talk to someone besides Frau Gothel." She carefully uncoils her braid from her arm and gently slips it back out the window.

I stick my head outside. "Come on up, Jonah!" I holler.

Immediately, my brother jumps up onto the braid, holding Prince under one arm. Unlike me, he seems to be trying the advanced method.

I hop off the ledge into the room, and Rapunzel sits back down in her chair. I take a closer look at her. She is really pretty. She has creamy dark skin, big brown eyes, and the longest eyelashes I've ever seen. Which isn't that surprising, considering how long her hair is.

Then I take a look around. So this is the infamous tower. Wow.

It's bigger than I expected: about twenty feet wide, and painted white. There's a green carpet on the floor, plus a cot, dresser, desk, and full-length mirror. A bookcase stands in one corner, and in the other is a small bathtub with little claw feet. I have always wanted a tub like that! So cute.

Beside the tub is a shelf lined with combs, brushes, and multiple small glass bottles filled with different colored liquids. Light blue, creamy white, pale pink. Those must be the fancy shampoos and conditioners Rapunzel mentioned.

I can't believe she lives in here. I'm ninety-nine percent sure I would go bonkers.

I notice that all around the room are also homemade instruments. A drum made out of a tin can. Five glasses of water set out like a xylophone. A shaker made out of an empty shampoo bottle. I guess that's how she keeps busy. Singing, reading, and making music.

Rapunzel grimaces, and I realize Jonah is still climbing up her braid.

"Are you okay?" I ask. "Does it always hurt?"

"A little," she admits. "It tugs on my scalp. But — ouch — this time it's hurting more than usual. Don't worry, I'm okay."

Maybe Jonah's advanced technique isn't the best idea.

A few seconds later, Jonah's and Prince's heads pop into view. "That was fun!" Jonah cries. He jumps over the ledge.

"It's a puppy!" Rapunzel exclaims, bending toward Prince. "Hello, puppy, hello."

Prince yips and tries to paw Rapunzel's braid.

Rapunzel giggles, but then nervously starts coiling the braid around her arm again. "Um, your puppy is very cute, but would you mind keeping him from my braid? My hair is really important to me and I need to be extra careful with it. . . ."

"Sit, Prince, sit!" I say, but of course he doesn't listen.

"Sorry, sorry," Jonah says, picking up Prince and pulling him away from the braid.

"Rapunzel," I begin, "meet my brother, Jonah, and our dog, Prince. Jonah and Prince, meet Rapunzel. I'm Abby, by the way. Did I already say that?"

"Hello," Rapunzel says, and continues coiling her hair around her arm. "It is really nice to have visitors. I wish you could stay longer, but Frau —" She freezes. Her eyes widen. She studies her braid, flips it, and runs her fingers over it. "Oh, no. Something happened to my hair."

"What do you mean?" I ask.

She runs her fingers over the strands. "It's all messed up."

I take a step closer and look. It does seem to be kind of frizzy. No — more than frizzy. It's a mess. Locks are broken and ripped. It looks like a wolf attacked it with its teeth. Is it possible the wolf from *Little Red Riding Hood* escaped from his story and climbed into this one? No way. Was it Prince? No. He's not the best listener but he couldn't have done that. It has to be something else.

"What happened?" I ask in shock. "Did I do that when I was climbing? It looks like someone hacked it with an ax! It looks like someone . . ." My voice trails off.

Oh, no.

He didn't.

He wouldn't.

I turn to my brother, who has been suspiciously silent. I look down at his shoes.

He did.

My brother climbed Rapunzel's hair wearing his soccer cleats.

# ✳ chapter five ✳

## Brushing Isn't Going to Help

a loud sob escapes Rapunzel's lips. "What happened to my hair? It was so pretty!"

It really *was* pretty. And now it's not. Now it looks like cheese that's been grated to make a pizza.

"Jonah!" I snap. "You DO realize that this is your fault, don't you?"

He blushes. "Mine? Why?"

"Your soccer cleats! You wore them while you climbed her hair!"

"He did this to me?" Rapunzel asks, whimpering.

Jonah's face is now the color of a very ripe tomato. "I'm s-sorry!" he stammers. "I didn't realize . . ."

"You didn't realize that your cleats would rip apart her hair?" I yell. "Mom said you couldn't even wear them in the house!"

"That's because she doesn't want me to ruin the shoes! Not because of the floors." He kicks up his toes. "These aren't even metal. They're just plastic!"

"Well, the plastic pulled on the strands," I say.

Rapunzel looks like she's desperately trying to blink back tears. "My hair was the only thing I had that was special," she murmurs.

"I'm really sorry," Jonah mumbles. "It was an accident."

"Let's try brushing it," I say, giving my brother a dirty look. "Jonah, get me a brush from the shelf near the bathtub. Let's take out the ribbon at the end and see what we have."

With trembling fingers, Rapunzel delicately searches for the end of the braid. She unties the ribbon. Multiple pieces of hair fall to the floor.

She gasps. We all gasp.

"I can't believe this. I am . . . so . . . so . . . mad at you," she says finally.

"At me?" I ask, feeling wounded. "It wasn't my fault!"

"You told me to let your brother up," she manages between tears.

"I know, but . . ." Ugh. I have to make this better! Rapunzel seems sweet and a little shy. And here she is locked up in the tower, and I ruined the one thing she clearly feels very good about. I grab the brush out of Jonah's hands. "Let me see what I can do. Turn around."

She bites her lip. "All right. But please don't make it worse."

"I won't! It'll look better if we get rid of the broken parts," I say hopefully. "Do you have a pair of scissors?"

Rapunzel cocks her head to the side. "I have nail scissors. What are you going to do with scissors?"

"I'm going to give you a trim," I say. I can't believe how long her hair is. "Have you *ever* cut your hair?"

"No. I love my hair the way it is." She sighs. "The way it *was*. Also, Frau Gothel said cutting it would hurt."

"She lied," I say. "It doesn't hurt at all. She doesn't want you to cut your hair because she needs it to climb up the tower."

Rapunzel's shoulders tense. She removes a pair of small scissors from her desk. "Then let's do it. Go ahead."

I nod. I crouch down to the floor and carefully raise the scissors to a piece of frizz by her foot. "Ready?"

She winces but nods.

I snip. The piece of broken hair cascades to the ground.

"That didn't hurt at all," Rapunzel gasps, her eyes widening. "I can't believe she lied to me. I can't believe I believed her. She told me she only cuts her own hair once a year because of the pain."

I snip away another piece of frizz. And another. It's looking much better already. Another snip. Another. Jonah is silent, obviously still feeling guilty, while Prince sniffs around the unfamiliar room.

"Are you sure you know what you're doing?" Rapunzel asks, trying to look behind her.

"Of course," I say reassuringly. "It's really not that hard." I've been to the hairdresser a million times, haven't I? At least once every six months. And there were all those dolls I practiced on!

A small mound of hair is piling up on the carpet.

Snip, snip, snip.

This is fun!

Prince thinks so, too. He nose-dives into the pile and plays in it like it's a bag of confetti.

Snip. Snip, snip.

Hey, I'm pretty good at this. Maybe I should be a hairdresser when I grow up. Nah, I really want to be a judge. Well, first I'm going to be a lawyer, and then I'm going to be a judge, because that's the rule. But I'm going to be an excellent judge. I'm very good at deciding what's fair. I am also excellent at telling people what to do.

Perhaps I can be a hairdresser in my spare time? Or as a hobby?

I cut a little bit more and then turn her around. I look Rapunzel straight in the eye. "Do you know what would look great on you?"

"What?" she asks.

"Bangs!"

"What are bangs?"

"You'll see!" I tell her cheerfully. Snip, snip, snip!

I can do this. I really can! Let me just even out the ends a little. I am doing a great job. So what if I messed up the spelling bee? That doesn't mean I'm not good at *other* stuff. Like haircutting. I am SO good at haircutting. Who cares that I'm not good at spelling? I don't. So what if I couldn't spell *cinnamon*? I don't even like cinnamon. I will never use it again. Ever. Not even on French toast.

"Abby," Jonah says, interrupting my thoughts. "Maybe you should stop? You cut *a lot*."

Huh? I did?

"Also, I think Prince is munching on the extra hair," Jonah adds.

"How much is a lot?" Rapunzel asks nervously.

I take a step back. Her hair still looks kind of bumpy. "I think I need to even it out some more," I say.

Snip. Snip —

Rapunzel blocks me with her hands. "Hold on. I should see before you cut any more. Jonah, can you please hand me that mirror?"

"Sure," he says, and takes it off the shelf.

"I'm not finished yet," I say as my brother hands the mirror to Rapunzel.

When she sees her reflection, her face crumples.

Uh-oh. I swallow. Hard.

Rapunzel's face turns bright red. "WHAT. DID. YOU. DO?"

Her hair is shoulder length. Actually, the right side is shoulder length. The left side is at her chin. The back looks a bit like a staircase, connecting the two lengths. And the bangs . . .

The bangs weren't my best idea.

My heart sinks. "I wasn't finished! Let me finish!"

"You are not allowed to touch my hair again!" Rapunzel yells, shielding her head with her hands.

"It's not that bad," I lie.

Jonah giggles while looking horrified. "It *is* that bad. It really is!"

I poke my brother in the shoulder. "Well, it's better than it was before! You were the one who climbed up her hair in soccer cleats!" But now I'm starting to doubt myself and my haircutting capabilities. So now I'm a bad speller and a bad haircutter?

Am I good at anything?

Prince spits out a chunk of hair.

"The cleats were an accident!" Jonah hollers.

Prince shoves another pawful of hair into his mouth.

"Still your fault!" I holler at Jonah. "Prince, sit and stop eating Rapunzel's hair!"

Prince makes a sad face. Then he sits. *Finally.* I knew he was trained.

Rapunzel tosses the mirror onto her bed and buries her face in her hands. "It's horrible. It's ruined. And it's all I had."

I know her new haircut isn't great, but isn't she being a wee bit overdramatic? "It's hair," I grumble. "It'll grow back. You're still beautiful."

Jonah taps me on the shoulder. "Abby?"

"What?" I snap.

He twists his lower lip. "I have a question."

"Now's not the time for a question, Jonah!"

He motions to the piles of hair all over the floor. "Now that Rapunzel's hair is short, how is Pickles going to use it to climb up to see her?"

Oh, no. Oh no oh no. I do not have an answer to that question. My head starts to pound. I rub my fingers against my temples.

"That is probably something you should have brought up before we broke out the nail scissors, Jonah!"

Rapunzel lifts her head. "Who's Pickles?"

I lean against the wall for support. "He means the prince. The prince who hears you singing and falls in love with you. And you fall in love back."

I brace myself for barking, but it seems that Prince is too busy stuffing his mouth with hair to notice.

Rapunzel wrinkles her brow. "That never happened. I would never sing in front of a prince. I would never sing in front of anyone. My songs aren't any good."

"They are good! And you didn't know he was listening. But he climbs up every night to see you. Well, that was what was *supposed* to happen. Until my brother messed everything up."

"You're the one who went crazy with the scissors," Jonah grumbles.

Rapunzel takes a deep, sad breath. "So you two messed up my future as well as my hair?"

I nod, glumly.

"But how do you even know the future?" she asks, gazing at us suspiciously.

"Where we come from, your story is famous," Jonah explains. "You and the prince —"

"*Ruff, ruff!*"

"— live happily ever after," Jonah goes on, petting Prince. "Well, eventually. First he goes blind and stuff."

Rapunzel looks confused, then shakes her head. "Even if he was going to fall in love with me, he won't now. Look at me." She points to her hair. "I'm hideous. No one would love someone with such hideous hair."

"That's crazy," I say. "First of all, your haircut isn't *that* bad."

"Is so," Jonah mumbles.

I shoot him a glare. "And second of all, the prince —"

"*Ruff, ruff!*"

"Pickles doesn't love you just for your hair. He loves you for you."

Rapunzel scrunches her nose. "What's so special about me?"

"I don't know you that well yet," I say. "But you seem sweet. And you're creative. You write your own songs. And make your own instruments."

"I bet you're fun to hang out with," Jonah adds.

"I have no idea if I'm fun to hang out with," Rapunzel says, her eyes full of tears again. "The only person I ever talk to is Frau Gothel, and she doesn't spend a lot of time with me. This is the most time I've ever spent with other people!"

"This?" I ask, motioning to myself and Jonah.

She nods.

We really need to think of a way to get the prince to meet her. Otherwise, she'll be lonely forever.

Or not.

Suddenly, I realize that the prince is not our only problem.

Problem #1: Rapunzel's braid is gone. The prince can't climb up. He has no way in.

Problem #2: Rapunzel's braid is gone. We can't climb down. We have no way out.

# ✳ chapter six ✳

## No Hair to Let Down

**h**ow are we going to get out of here?" I ask, glancing around nervously. I'm already starting to feel claustrophobic. I'm a growing girl — I need my space! I can't live in a tower. Let me out, let me out!

Prince starts to howl. Clearly, he can sense my pain. Such a sensitive dog. Or maybe he just needs to go outside for *other* reasons.

Uh-oh.

"What do we do?" Jonah asks.

I look down at all the hair on the floor. "Maybe we can weave a rope?"

"With scraps of hair?" Rapunzel asks. "I don't think so."

"Rapunzel!" We hear a woman's voice from outside. "Rapunzel! Let down your hair!"

Prince's ears perk up.

I freeze. Oh, boy.

Jonah sneaks a look outside. "It's an old woman on a horse," he reports, confirming my fear. "It must be Frown!"

"Frau," I correct. "Frau Gothel. The witch." My heart starts racing.

Rapunzel nods, looking terrified. "Yes, she must be here on her horse, Basil."

"What if she uses her magic to cast spells on all of us?" I ask in a panic.

Prince howls again.

"Shhh!" Rapunzel begs. "Make him be quiet. We can't let her hear the dog! She'll turn him into a toad!"

"Calm down, Prince, calm down," Jonah whispers. "She named her horse *Basil*? That's the worst name for a horse I ever heard."

"She must really like herbs," I say.

"She's going to be *really* upset that I cut my hair," Rapunzel moans, pulling at her locks. "She said I shouldn't even try. And she'll also be furious that I let you two — you *three* — up. She said I should never let anyone up. What do I do?"

"Come on, Rapunzel, let down your hair!" Frau Gothel hollers.

I lower my voice and duck out of sight. "Don't tell her we're here. But you have to tell her you cut your hair. You don't have much of a choice."

Rapunzel leans her head out the window. "Hi, Frau Gothel."

"What's taking you so long?" the witch snaps. "Let down your hair already! It's hot in the sun!"

"I have a bit of a problem. I . . . um . . . cut it?" Rapunzel says it like a question.

"YOU WHAT?" Frau Gothel yells. "Why would you do something so stupid?"

Rapunzel twists what's left of her hair between her fingers and turns to us. "I don't know," she whispers, her eyes wide with fear. "What's a good answer here?"

"Because . . . because . . ." I don't know, either!

"Because you got gum in it!" Jonah exclaims. "That happened to a girl in my class. Isaac accidentally spit out his piece of gum and it landed on the back of her head and —"

"What's gum?" Rapunzel asks, blinking.

"You don't have gum in this kingdom?" Jonah asks, looking pained. "Not even bubble gum?"

"No."

"What about peanut butter?" Jonah asks. "Prince really likes peanut butter. Also pumpkin seeds. He's probably pretty hungry."

Prince is now rolling around on the carpet, which is his way of asking one of us to rub his belly.

I rub it. He pants happily.

"RAPUNZEL!" Frau Gothel yells. "Tell me why you cut your hair!"

Rapunzel sticks her head out the window again. "I was hot!"

"Good answer," I whisper. "I would totally buy that. It's very stuffy in here."

"When I get up there, you will be punished!" Frau Gothel hollers. "I'll — I'll — I'll shrink you to the size of a fingernail!

You will regret your behavior, Rapunzel! My pets will not disobey me!"

Pets?

Rapunzel pulls away from the window, trembling. "I don't want to be the size of a fingernail," she whispers.

"Maybe it's a really long fingernail?" Jonah says. "Don't witches have really long nails?"

I scoop up Prince and clutch him to my chest.

"Does Frau Gothel have another way up?" I ask Rapunzel. "Like a broom?" I wish I could see the witch's face and how she's reacting to all this, but I'm standing as far away as I can from the window.

"I'm sorry, Frau Gothel," Rapunzel calls down. "Please forgive me?"

I hold my breath, waiting to hear the witch's response. Can she fly? Will she really shrink us? Or turn us into frogs? Or toads?

What's the difference between a toad and a frog exactly?

We wait. Nothing happens.

"All right," the witch calls up eventually. "I'll be back. I'm going to get a ladder. Giddyup, Basil." We hear a horse neigh and trot away.

Rapunzel stares out the window. "She's going. She's going. She's gone," she reports. She turns back to us. "Now what? When she climbs up, she'll find you all here!"

Jonah puts his hands on his hips. "I can't believe she's getting a ladder."

"Why?" Rapunzel asks, sitting on the edge of her bed. "How did you expect her to get up?"

"I thought she was a witch," Jonah says. "I expected her to fly."

I can't help but agree. "A ladder does seem pretty un-witchlike."

"Trust me," Rapunzel says. "She's a witch."

Hmm. I set Prince down and cross my arms. "Has she ever put spells on you?"

"Yes," Rapunzel says, nodding. "She put a spell on me that stops me from leaving the tower."

"What happens if you try to leave?" I ask. It would have to be something really bad to get *me* to stay here.

"She said all of my teeth would fall out," Rapunzel says, and then slams her mouth shut.

I shiver. "That's horrible."

"It would definitely make eating hard," Jonah says. "Although you could still slurp stuff. Like peanut butter. Or ice cream. And ketchup. And ketchup-flavored ice cream."

I roll my eyes. "Jonah, that is not a thing."

"It should be a thing. Yum." He licks his lips and then turns back to Rapunzel. "Have you ever *tried* to leave?"

She shakes her head. "Of course not. I don't want to lose my teeth. I like my teeth. I especially can't lose my teeth now that I've lost my hair."

"You haven't lost your hair," I grumble. "Well, just some of it."

Jonah crouches down and scratches Prince behind the ears. "But, Rapunzel, how do you know Frown *really* cast the spell?"

"What do you mean?" Rapunzel asks, sitting back down on her chair. "She told me she did."

Where's Jonah going with this?

"Did you see any sparkles?" he asks. "Or puffs of smoke or anything like that?"

Rapunzel shakes her head.

"Then how do you know she's really a witch?" my brother asks.

"Because she said she was a witch," Rapunzel answers.

We both stare at Jonah blankly.

"But have you ever seen her do any *actual* magic?" Jonah presses.

"You're saying she's not really a witch?" I ask, amazed.

Jonah nods. "Yup. That's exactly what I'm saying."

"But she wears all black," Rapunzel says. "She calls herself a witch, too."

Jonah shakes his head. "She sounds like a *wannabe* witch," he pronounces.

Oh my gosh. My brother is totally right.

"I think Jonah has a point!" I exclaim.

But hadn't the original story *said* Frau Gothel was a witch? Although sometimes the fairy tale we visit isn't exactly the same as the version Nana told us or the one I read in my school library. And sometimes I remember stuff wrong. There are so many stories and so many details!

Rapunzel's eyes grow large. "You're saying that there's no spell on me? You're saying I can leave the tower anytime I want?"

Jonah nods. "If there's no spell, then yeah."

"I am not staying here one second longer than I have to," Rapunzel says, jumping up from the chair. "Let's go!"

"Wait, wait, wait," I say. "If you leave, the story won't continue the way it's supposed to."

Jonah shakes his head. "Abby, the story won't continue the way it's supposed to anyway. Pickles can't climb up Rapunzel's hair anymore! But if we escape, maybe she can meet him *outside* the tower instead of inside it."

"That's true," I say, thinking fast. "We do know Pickles comes by the tower eventually. If we wait downstairs, he'll show up. Except . . ." I feel a pinprick of anxiety. "There's no way out of here. Remember?"

Prince howls in agreement.

"Right," Jonah says, scrunching his nose. "That's still a problem."

Hmm. I need to think. I start to pace around the room. "If Frau is just a wannabe witch, there must be another way in and out of the tower."

"Why?" Jonah asks.

"Because," I say, "how did Rapunzel get in to begin with? She couldn't climb her own hair."

"Good point," Jonah says.

"Maybe we used the ladder," Rapunzel adds.

"Don't you remember?" I ask her.

She shakes her head. "I don't. All I know is, one night when I was twelve, I went to bed at her house, as usual . . . and then, when I woke up, I was here. She must have moved me when I was asleep."

"Then she could have used her ladder and carried you up," I admit. "But why would anyone build a tower with no door? It makes no sense."

"You're right," Jonah says. His face lights up. "I bet there's a secret door."

"I don't know," I say doubtfully. "If there was a secret door, wouldn't Frau Gothel have used it now? Why would she go get a ladder if she knew there was a secret door?"

Jonah rolls his eyes. "Because she doesn't want Rapunzel to *know* about the secret door. Duh. She doesn't want Rapunzel to leave. I bet she doesn't leave the ladder behind, either. She'll use it, and then move it so that Rapunzel stays trapped."

"Interesting," I say, tapping my fingers against my leg.

"Let's look for the door!" my brother cries, glancing around.

"If I were a secret door, where would I be?" I wonder.

"Don't you think I would have noticed a secret door?" Rapunzel asks. She sits back down on the chair.

"No," Jonah says. "That's the whole point of secret doors. They're secret!"

I take in the whole room. The dresser. Desk. Bookcase. Tub. Aren't secret doors usually behind large pieces of furniture?

"Let's check behind the bookcase," Jonah says, clearly thinking the same thing.

I walk over to the shelves. They're stuffed full of books, as well as spiral-bound notebooks. "What are these?" I ask, pointing to the notebooks.

Rapunzel blushes. "My poems. Well, songs. Poems that I turn into songs."

"That's amazing!" I tell her, meaning it. I've never met anyone who writes songs. "C'mon, guys, let's move this thing."

Together, Rapunzel, Jonah, and I take different sides of the bookcase. We pull and we push.

All the books spill onto the floor. Prince howls in delight.

"Oops," I say.

Rapunzel shrugs. "It's okay. There's lots of time to clean up around here. I don't have anything else to do. Sometimes I knock my books off just for fun."

Poor Rapunzel.

We look behind the bookcase. No secret door.

We search behind the dresser and the desk and the bed.

There are no secret doors anywhere. My spirits sink.

"It has to be here somewhere!" Jonah cries.

"I told you I would have *noticed* a secret door," Rapunzel grumbles. "So what do we do now? We're stuck!"

"Maybe we could jump out the window," Jonah offers.

"We are not jumping out the window," I say firmly. "It's too high. And there are those thorny bushes. That's how Pickles goes blind in the story."

*"Ruff, ruff!"*

"I said Pickles," I tell Prince, wagging my finger. "Why are you barking?"

*"Ruff, ruff!"*

Prince digs his nose into the middle of the carpet. Then scratches the carpet with his paw, as though he's digging for a bone.

Is he trying to tell me something?

I feel a flash of inspiration.

He is!

I drop to my knees and study the green carpet. "Have you ever looked underneath?" I ask Rapunzel.

She shakes her head.

Jonah claps his hands together gleefully. "It's there! It's there for sure!"

We roll up the old, faded carpet and, lo and behold, right under where Prince was sniffing is a whole lot of dust and the outline of a small wooden hatch.

# ✳ chapter seven ✳

## Decisions, Decisions

**g**ood boy, good boy!" I tell Prince, ruffling his fur.

"I knew there was a door!" Jonah exclaims triumphantly.

"But there's no handle," I say, biting my lip. "How can we open it? Someone pass me the scissors."

Rapunzel hesitates. "You may have lost your scissors privileges."

"Oh, come on!"

"Fine," she says. "But you have to stay at least two feet away from me while you're holding them." She passes them to me at arm's length.

I roll my eyes. Carefully, I stick the scissors in the hatch, wiggle them around, and then—pop! The door in the floor springs open and reveals a spiral staircase below.

"Oh, wow," Rapunzel breathes.

"Definite wow," I say.

Jonah cheers. "But wouldn't it have been better if it was a fireman's pole?"

I shake my head. "Jonah, that doesn't make any sense. How could Frau Gothel have climbed *up* a fireman's pole?"

"I bet I could climb up a fireman's pole. Do you think Mom would get one for our house? We could cut a hole in the kitchen floor, and it would go right into the basement."

"No, I do not," I say. Sometimes my brother lives in a fantasy world. "Come on, guys, let's go. Rapunzel, why don't you go first?"

"Me?" she asks, her shoulders clenching.

"Yeah!"

"But . . ."

"But what?" I ask, impatient. Frau could be back any second! For the first time since I've been here, I glance at my watch. It still says midnight. Does that mean no time has passed back in Smithville? Weird. In any case, we have to get moving. I am filled with energy even though I should probably be exhausted. The exhaustion will kick in eventually. Hopefully when there is no longer a wannabe witch chasing us.

She pales. "B-but what if Frau *is* a witch? I like my teeth!"

"She's a wannabe witch," Jonah insists.

I hesitate. "We don't know that *for sure*. . . ."

"If someone is a witch, they prove they're a witch," Jonah says, waving his arms in the air. "They do spells and stuff. They don't go home and get a ladder. All we know about Frown is that she's a nonmagical liar who keeps Rapunzel locked in a tower!"

"True," I say. "And, if she *is* a witch, she swore to turn you into a toad when she gets back. Wouldn't you rather lose your teeth than be turned into a toad?"

Rapunzel sighs. "I guess so."

"My friend Isaac's dad is a dentist," Jonah pipes up. "You could come back to Smithville with us and he'd get you dentures!"

She contemplates the offer. "Will I have to live in a tower in Smithville?"

"No," Jonah says. "You could live in a house. You'll share Abby's room. She's always wanted bunk beds."

I shoot my brother a look. "She can't come back to Smithville with us!"

"Why not?" Jonah asks. "We brought Prince home with us."

"Prince is a dog. She's a Rapunzel!" Although I *have* always wanted bunk beds. "Look, Rapunzel," I say to her, "let's go outside. We'll find Pickles and we'll skip straight to the end of the story. You'll still live happily ever after."

Rapunzel bites her thumbnail. "But . . ."

"But what?" I ask.

Rapunzel motions around the room. "This is where I've lived for so long. All my stuff is here! My poems! My books! My instruments! All my hair gels and conditioners!"

"You'll write new poems. You can get more hair products."

We hear a voice outside. "I'm back!" the wannabe witch calls out. There's a bang against the side of the tower. "And you, Rapunzel, you are going to regret cutting your hair. I promise you that," she snarls.

Fear shoots through me. "We have to move NOW! Jonah, go first."

Jonah salutes us and disappears down the hole to the stairs.

I pick up Prince and hug him to my chest. I'm afraid he might try to jump, but instead he licks my neck.

"Rapunzel, go next," I say.

She hesitates. "But . . . I don't even know you guys!"

"Trust me, you'd rather be with us than with an angry wannabe witch who just vowed to punish you. Even if she doesn't have magical powers, she can still do bad stuff. I mean, she's kept you locked in a tower for years!"

"Yeah," Jonah exclaims from the staircase below. "She could hang you out of the window by your toes. Or cut *off* your toes. Like Cinderella's stepsisters!"

Gross. "Thanks for the visual, Jonah."

"But . . ." Rapunzel's eyes refill with tears. "My hair is gone. I don't want anyone to see me!"

"It is not gone. It's just short. Anyway, no one could see you even when you had hair. Because you were hidden away." Holding Prince, I squeeze my way into the open hatch and start down the stairs. "Follow me. You'll be safer with us."

I really, really hope I'm not wrong.

I really, really hope she doesn't lose her teeth.

But Frau Gothel will be showing up any minute.

Rapunzel hesitates again. She glances over to the window and then down at me. She takes a big breath, climbs down onto the stairs, and closes the latch behind her.

*Whew.*

We go around and around down the steps. Jonah finds the door to outside. He struggles to push it open. There are thorn-bushes blocking it, so it doesn't open all the way. Just enough for him to squeeze out.

I squish my way out next and look up. I can see Frau Gothel standing on top of the ladder and wedging her top half through the open window. She's wearing black overalls. Also black rubber rain boots. The outfit reminds me of what my nana wears for gardening, except my nana's overalls are denim and her boots are pink.

Not the best shoes to climb a ladder in, if you ask me. But at least they're better than soccer cleats.

I turn back to Rapunzel, who's still at the foot of the stairs, just inside the tower. "Ready to come out?" I whisper.

She licks her teeth protectively. "I guess. Here goes nothing."

She holds her breath and steps outside, into the air and sunlight.

"Rapunzel?" I ask nervously. "Are you okay?" *Please still have teeth, please still have teeth.*

She smiles. Her teeth gleam. "Still got 'em."

Jonah and I raise our arms in a silent cheer. Prince, thankfully, does not bark. He is too busy relieving himself under a tree.

From above us and inside the tower, Frau Gothel calls out, "Rapunzel, why is it so messy in here? Rapunzel? Where are you?"

I feel another surge of fear. "I don't think staying here and waiting for Pickles is an option," I whisper. "Maybe we should go meet him at his palace?"

"Good idea!" Jonah says.

I grab both Rapunzel's and my brother's hands. "Run!"

We run, Prince at our heels.

Rapunzel huffs and puffs as we go. I guess she hasn't done much running lately, which is understandable. It's not like she had a treadmill in the tower.

"Where do we go?" Rapunzel asks, out of breath. "Oh my goodness, it's so beautiful out here! I forgot how soft the ground is! I haven't been outside in three years."

The ground does not feel particularly soft to me, but I guess compared to the tower's stone floor, the regular earth is soft as a feather bed. I look around, taking in the surroundings. It really is pretty. The tower is in a small valley surrounded by hills that are covered in tall bushy trees. That must be why no one ever saw the tower.

"Let's go back up to the hills!" Jonah suggests, charging ahead.

As we sprint up to the forest, I ask, "Rapunzel, which way is the palace?"

"I have no idea," Rapunzel says between huffs.

I stop in my tracks. Prince crashes into my ankle. "We should stop running if we don't know where we're going. I think we're far enough away from the wannabe witch."

"So you don't know where we're going, either?" Rapunzel asks, frowning.

"How would we? We just arrived in this kingdom a few hours ago." I sigh. "This is a real problem."

"Yes," Jonah says. Then he smirks. "It's a real quandary. You know how to spell that, right, Abby?"

I narrow my eyes. "Yes, Jonah. Q-U-A-N-D-E-R-Y."

His lips curl into a smile. "You sure it's not Q-U-A-N-D . . . *A*-R-Y?"

Oh, no. He's right! It is an *A*. My cheeks burn. "How did you know that?"

A huge smile spreads across his face. "You're wrong? I'm right?"

"JONAH, HOW DID YOU KNOW THAT?"

He shrugs. "I'm smart."

"Did you look that up?"

"I might have. Or maybe I'm just a genius. Maybe I'll be the spelling bee champion in school this year. I'm definitely the spelling bee champion of our family."

"I'm the spelling bee champion of our family!" I snap, my blood boiling.

"Not anymore," he taunts.

"If you're so smart, why don't you come up with a plan to find the castle for us?" I ask him sharply. "In the real story, Rapunzel and the prince wandered around for years until they found each other. YEARS. We can't be lost in the forest for years! We'll starve! And we have to get home!" I glance at my watch, which still says twelve. Could time really be passing *that* slowly at home? Has not even a full minute gone by? Did I break my watch when we went through the mirror?

"Don't worry," Jonah says smugly. "I do have a genius plan. Wanna hear?"

## chapter eight

## No Parriage in Sight

guess so," I say with a sigh, still angry about his *quandary* teasing.

Jonah points to a tall tree in the distance. "We climb up one of the trees and try to spot the palace. This way we can also keep an eye on the tower, to see if the wannabe witch leaves or if Pickles arrives."

"You know how to climb *trees*?" Rapunzel asks, eyes wide.

Jonah nods proudly.

"Can you show me?"

"Of course!" Jonah says. "Abby knows, too. We've done it before. We can all climb together!"

We make our way over to the highest tree, and Jonah rubs his hands together eagerly.

"Prince, you stay here," I order. "Stay!"

Luckily, Prince decides to take the opportunity to chase his tail in a circle.

Jonah and I jump up to reach a branch. I hold on to one branch and climb higher and higher. I really have gotten so much better at climbing since we started going through the mirror. If only my class held a climbing trees bee instead of a spelling bee.

Rapunzel isn't as sure-footed as we are, but soon she starts climbing up, too. She gets the hang of it pretty quickly. Her eyes are twinkling and she looks excited just to be in the outside world.

"Whoa!" Jonah exclaims when he gets to the top.

When I join him, I gasp. It's an amazing view. In the distance, there are more mountains covered in trees, and dazzling waterfalls spilling into blue lakes. There are also dirt roads zigzagging in and around. But the most amazing thing about the view is that there is a haze of multicolored sparkles hovering over the mountains.

"Why are the mountains twinkling?" I wonder.

"It's the sunlight bouncing off the kingdom's gemstones," Rapunzel explains. "And you can only see it from a distance."

"Gemstones?" I wonder.

She nods. "Generations and generations ago, a wealthy traveler named Tristan discovered that this land had an abundance of gems in the rocks and mountains. Diamonds. Emeralds. Sapphires. Amethysts. He brought a group down to mine them, declared himself king, and took possession of all the jewels. He named the kingdom Glimmer after the haze. Frau Gothel gave me a book about it."

"How do you spell Glimmer?" Jonah asks.

"G-L-I-M-M-E-R," Rapunzel says.

"You're a good speller, Rapunzel," my brother says.

My back tightens. "Glimmer is an easy word. I could have spelled it, too."

Jonah turns back to Rapunzel. "Can you spell 'cinnamon'?"

"C-I-N-N-A-M-O-N."

" 'Quandary'?" he asks.

"Q-U-A-N-D-A-R-Y." She shrugs. "I spend a lot of time reading my dictionary."

Humph. Of course she's a better speller than I am — she's older than me.

I don't want to talk about spelling anymore.

I glance back at the view. "I don't see a castle, do you?"

"No," they both say.

"What's that blue thing?" Jonah asks, pointing.

The blue thing he's pointing to is moving. Also, it's being led by a small brown dot. Oh! It's a horse!

"I think it's a carriage!" I exclaim. "Oh, look. I see an orange one, too. There are a bunch of carriages."

"Let's go." Jonah starts to climb back down the tree. "I bet one of them can take us to the palace."

"Jonah," I say. "You know we're not supposed to ask strangers for rides."

He frowns. "Oh, right. So what do we do?"

"Well," I say. "Maybe a parriage will drive by."

"Just like in *Cinderella*?" Jonah asks.

"Exactly."

Rapunzel shifts her weight on the branch. "What's a parriage?"

"A public carriage," I say. "Like a bus."

She blinks. "What's a bus?"

"A kind of carriage that takes anyone who pays."

She scrunches her eyebrows. "I don't think I've heard about either of those things."

"Then I guess you don't know everything," I mutter.

"Sorry?" she asks. "I missed what you said."

"Nothing," I say.

"Jealous," Jonah says. "J-E-L-O-S."

"Wrong," I tell him.

He smiles. "Close enough."

The three of us carefully shimmy back down the tree. Then, with Prince scurrying along beside us, we hike over to the road where I saw the carriages.

The walk takes what feels like an hour, but my watch still says twelve o'clock. I am worried it is broken. I am also worried about Rapunzel's feet because she is not wearing any shoes. I am worried about a lot of things.

We wait by the side of the road, and a bunch of carriages pass by, but Rapunzel was right. There are no parriages in Glimmer.

Which causes us a bit of a problem. How are we going to get to the palace if we can't ask someone for a lift?

A carriage drives up and stops in front of us. The sight of a horse so close by makes Prince bark like a maniac.

The driver, a jolly old man, looks like the Santa at the mall. He even has a gray beard.

"Hello there," he booms. "Do you guys need a lift?"

"Yes," Rapunzel says.

"No, thank you," I say. "But can you tell us how to get to the palace?"

"Sure. It's about a two-hour ride that way." He points ahead to the twisty road.

"But do we turn right at the fork or left?"

"Left," he says. "And then right. And then right and then left and then right. Are you sure you don't want a lift?"

"Yes," I say unhappily.

"Good luck!" he says, and rides away.

"Now what?" Jonah asks. "We can't walk. We'll get lost for sure. Plus, a two-hour ride would take us a day to walk. At least."

I glance down at Rapunzel's feet. They're looking a little beat-up. I don't think she can walk for that much longer. What are we going to do?

*Badoom! Badoom! Badoom!*

The sound of hooves makes me glance back up. A horse is coming down the road, pulling a bright yellow carriage. On the side of the carriage, it says HAXI.

"What's a haxi?" Jonah wonders.

"Could it be . . . a horse taxi?" I wonder aloud. Yes! Yes! I bet it is! I wave to the driver, a lady wearing a purple dress.

The lady slows down. Prince barks and jumps. "Where to?" the driver asks.

"Are you a horse taxi?" I ask.

"No, I'm a *haxi* driver," she says.

This driver does not look like Santa Claus at all. Or even Mrs. Claus. Her hair is bright red and spiky and she's rail thin. She's also wearing round black glasses that cover most of her face.

"Does that mean you take people where they want to go and charge them?" Jonah asks.

She nods. "Yup."

"Hurray!" I cheer. "A horse taxi!"

"A haxi," she repeats.

"Perfect," Rapunzel says. "Let's get in."

"Where are you going?" the haxi driver asks. She stares at Rapunzel. "What happened to your hair?"

Rapunzel flushes.

I cough loudly. "We're going to the palace."

The woman nods. "That will be one sapphire."

One sapphire? They pay in gems?

"Done!" Jonah says.

"Jonah, I don't have any *sapphires* on me. I don't have any sapphires at all. Do you?"

He shakes his head.

We turn to Rapunzel. "Do you have any sapphires?" I ask.

She shakes her head.

Prince wags his tail.

"No sapphires, no haxi," the driver says, and picks up the reins as though she's about to take off.

"Wait!" I cry. "Can we pay with something else? Maybe we can trade you something?"

"Like what?" she asks. "Do you have any rubies? Emeralds? Diamonds?"

"Nope." I turn to the others. "What do you have that's worth anything?"

"I don't even have shoes," Rapunzel says. "Speaking of shoes, maybe Jonah should trade his. They caused some problems." She brings a self-conscious hand to her hair.

"But I just got them," he whines.

"But they're evil," Rapunzel says. "And we need to trade *something*."

Jonah sighs. "All right, I'll trade my cleats." He takes them off and offers them to the driver. "How about these?"

She shakes her head. "I don't want shoes with spikes on them. They'll ruin my floors."

"Exactly," I say.

"Can I have the dog?" the driver asks. "I've always wanted a dog."

Prince whimpers and hides behind my legs.

"Definitely not," I say, rubbing his fur with my ankle.

"Hang on. What's that?" the driver asks. She's pointing to my wrist.

"My watch," I say.

"It tells the time?" she exclaims.

Um, yeah. Isn't that what watches do? Wait. Maybe they don't have clocks in fairy tales. No, of course they have clocks. Didn't the clock strike twelve in *Cinderella*? Wait. I know! She's amazed because the watch face doesn't have hands. "It's digital," I explain.

"Does digital mean broken?" she scoffs. "What kind of watch says twelve when it's already three thirty?"

My stomach plummets, and I look at my wrist. The watch does say twelve o'clock. It can't possibly *still* be midnight in Smithville, can it? Is time passing that slowly? I'm starting to worry that my watch has, in fact, stopped working. Which means it could be *any time* at home. I feel a flash of panic. Then I try to tell myself everything will be fine. Jonah and I always make it back to Smithville before our parents wake up. We will now, too. Right?

That just means we have to move faster.

"My watch does other things, too!" I say quickly. At least, I hope it does. "Want to see something cool?" I fiddle with a few buttons. There's a loud beep. It might not be able to tell the time of day, but the *stopwatch* still works.

"Big deal," the haxi driver says. "My horse makes noises, too."

"It's a timer!" I explain frantically while Rapunzel and Jonah watch me hopefully. "You could time how long it takes you to get to the palace and then charge us based on that!"

She looks at me as if I'm crazy. "I already told you what I'm charging you — one sapphire. One sapphire that you don't seem to have."

This isn't going well. What else can my watch do? "Oh! Look! It has a light!" I press a button and the watch's face lights up. "Wouldn't that be helpful? Late at night?"

The haxi driver motions me closer. "Let me see."

I press the light button again.

Her eyes widen. "A magic light! That *would* be helpful. It's a deal. Give me the watch, and I'll take you to the palace."

I let out a big breath and exchange relieved glances with Rapunzel and Jonah. Even Prince looks relieved.

We have a deal.

# * chapter nine *

## Next

We drive up rocky mountain roads and down rocky mountain roads.

I try to sleep a bit, but driving on rocks is pretty bumpy, so as soon as my eyes close, they slam back open. Rapunzel is wide awake, too, but silent as she gazes out the window in wonder. Jonah and Prince must be exhausted, though, because they are both fast asleep, Prince is snoring away in Jonah's lap.

Finally, the haxi driver starts carefully maneuvering her way up a hill.

We pass rows of horses and carriages that seem to be empty

and stopped. Like they're parked. At the end of the road, there's a high stone wall. A beautiful sunset of red and orange shimmers against the gray stone ground. In the distance, I see more glittery haze. This kingdom is really pretty.

"We're here!" the driver calls. Jonah and Prince both wake with a start. "No haxis or carriages are allowed inside. You have to knock on the door and be let in." She points to the stone wall.

"Thanks so much!" I tell her. Prince leaps out first and runs straight to the wall. The rest of us slowly stretch and pile out of the haxi. "Enjoy the watch," I say. I feel a tightening in my stomach. I hope giving away the watch wasn't a big mistake.

"Oh, I will," she says before turning her haxi around and riding away.

The stone wall is about two stories high, with a knocker at eye level. I can see the top of the palace rising up behind the wall. The roof glistens. It's bright. Shiny. And very, very colorful.

Oh, wow. Could it be?

"Is the palace made of jewels?" I ask in awe.

"I think so," Rapunzel says.

There are rubies. Diamonds. Emeralds. All in pretty patterns, like a mosaic.

"Do *all* the people in this kingdom have a lot of jewels?" I ask Rapunzel.

"I don't," she says. "I've never seen a jewel in my life until now."

I bang the knocker.

"May I help you?" asks a man, opening the door. He looks like the guards I've seen in pictures of Buckingham Palace in England. Except his uniform is covered in glitter.

"Yes," I say. "You can. We're here to see Pick — I mean, the prince."

*"Ruff, ruff!"*

"Go ahead," the guard says, motioning us inside.

We go in. And gasp.

It really is a PALACE OF JEWELS.

Surrounding the palace are smaller stone buildings made of sapphires, rubies, and emeralds, and smaller stone passageways, all similarly colorful and sparkling. I can't stop gawking. I wish I had a camera. Although who could I show the pictures to back home?

There is a line of people snaking around the buildings all the way to the ruby castle door. They have sleeping bags with them. And chairs.

"People are camping out," Jonah says. "It's like they're trying to buy tickets to something. Maybe there's a concert at the palace?"

"What's a concert?" Rapunzel asks.

"You know, when people pay money to go see a singer?" Jonah says, scooping up Prince under his arm.

Rapunzel's eyes widen. "People pay money to see a singer?"

I nod. "Lots of people. My mom took me to a concert once, and there were thousands of people in the audience."

Rapunzel shudders. "Thousands? I never sing in front of anyone. Except you guys. But that was an accident."

An idea flashes through my head and I grin excitedly. "I know! You should sing for Pickles!"

She shakes her head fast. "Sing for a prince? I don't think so!" She puts her hands self-consciously to her newly shorn hair.

"But that's how he finds you in the story. He hears your voice. . . ." I try to explain but then trail off. I don't have to

90

convince her to sing this second. I just have to get her a face-to-face meeting. "Let's at least go talk to him."

We make our way past the many, many people. There are families and couples holding kids. They're dressed in worn clothes and tattered shoes. No jewels here. Definitely no one wearing diamond earrings or pearl necklaces.

We walk right up to another glitter-clad guard at the front door.

"Hello," I say in my most grown-up voice. "We'd like to see the prince!"

On cue, Prince barks happily in Jonah's arms.

The guard nods. "All right."

Hurray! I knew this was a good plan. "Should we just go in?"

He shakes his head. "Get in line."

*Huh?* "Line?"

"Yes," the guard says.

"What line?"

He motions to the hundreds of people behind us. "That line."

Rapunzel, Jonah, and I exchange shocked glances. "Are you kidding me?" I cry. "All those people are here to see the prince?"

Even my puppy is stunned — he doesn't bark at the sound of his name.

The glittery guard nods.

"But why?" Jonah asks.

He shrugs. "They want gems."

I look at the palace. "From the palace? Is the prince taking it apart?"

"No," he says. "The royal family has more."

"Okay," I say. "But we don't want gems. We just want to talk to him so he can meet Rapunzel." I gesture to Rapunzel, who ducks her head and blushes. "So can we see him?"

The guard cocks his head to the side. "Yes."

"Great!" Jonah cheers.

The guard smiles. His front tooth is missing and has been replaced by a diamond. "After you wait in line."

Prince howls. I feel his pain.

Slowly, we all wind our way back to the end of the line. Jonah sets down Prince, who starts sniffing the stone ground.

We stand behind a mom holding a baby. The baby is crying loudly and a little hysterically.

"Are you here to get gems?" I ask the exhausted-looking mother.

"Yes," she says. "Everyone is. The royal family has held on to the jewels for generations. They've been very stingy. They mine the ground and keep the gems for themselves."

Hmm. That doesn't sound very nice. Maybe Rapunzel doesn't want to get mixed up with this family after all.

"But," the mom continues, "King Tristan the Fifth has made a change recently. His dying wish is to distribute the gems to whoever is the neediest. We just have to line up here and ask for help. His son, Prince —"

I glance at Prince, but he's too busy sniffing his new surroundings to notice his name.

"Tristan, considers all of our requests. He's here every day from seven A.M. to nine at night, and he only takes one hour off for lunch. He's very generous. I'm asking him to give us some gems so we can buy a new rocking chair. And maybe some new baby clothes. We could really use the help. Little Emma here won't stop crying. And now it's already seven and she's so tired. . . ."

"Poor baby," Rapunzel murmurs. She looks over at me, takes a deep breath, and leans closer to the baby. She lowers her voice and sings:

*"Hello, moon; good night, sun,*
*Close your eyes, sweet little one.*
*Tomorrow will be another day,*
*Then we'll have time to play."*

The baby lets out a baby sigh, blinks twice, and falls fast asleep.

"That was amazing!" the mom gushes, looking at Rapunzel in wonder. "You have a lovely voice. And I've never heard that lullaby before. Where did you learn it?"

"I made it up," Rapunzel admits sheepishly.

"Do you mind if I use it?" the mom asks.

"I'd be honored," Rapunzel says, smiling. "No one has ever sung my songs before."

"How long do you think this line is?" Jonah asks. He's shifting his weight from side to side, clearly getting antsy.

"I'm guessing at least five days," the mom says. "That's why I brought a tent." She gestures to the backpack at her feet. "I'm going to set it up now that the baby is asleep."

Crumbs. Five days! We can't stay for five days. That would be WAY too much time back home. Not that I know for sure without my watch. I miss my watch. Even if it was broken.

"Where are we going to sleep?" Rapunzel asks us. "We don't have a tent!"

My shoulders slump. I'm starting to get tired. Fairy tale jet lag. I wish I could have slept in the haxi. "We can't stay here for five days. We don't have any food or anything."

Jonah shrugs. "Why don't we go to Rapunzel's house?"

"You mean the tower?" I ask incredulously. "The wannabe witch is there! Plus, it's two hours away."

"No, I mean Rapunzel's *real* house," Jonah says. "Where her parents live."

Her parents?

Her parents!

# * chapter ten *

## An Onion a Day

Rapunzel's eyes widen. "My parents are still alive?"

"Yes!" I say, trying to remember the fairy tale. "At least, I think they are. Did you think they were dead?"

"That's what Frau Gothel said." Rapunzel frowns. "That they died and that's why she had to take me."

"Not exactly . . ." I take a deep breath and then tell Rapunzel the whole story. I try to keep my voice low so the people on line around us won't hear.

Rapunzel closes her eyes. I can see the pain on her face. "I can't believe my dad traded me for an herb."

"If he hadn't, your mother would have died," I say softly.

"Or maybe he just didn't care about me," she whispers.

"That can't be it," I say. "He probably thought he didn't have a choice."

"I'm sure they'll be so happy to see you again!" Jonah says.

"You really think I can meet my parents?" Rapunzel asks, hope creeping into her voice.

I nod, suddenly energized. "Of course! Hey! Maybe *that* can be the happy ending to your story. Forget meeting the prince. You need to remeet your parents!"

Who cares about this crazy wait? Not us. We're out of here!

"But how will we find them?" Rapunzel asks before I can step out of the line. "I don't even know their names."

I rub my temples with my fingers. "Let's think."

"We know they live next door to Frown," Jonah says. "That was part of the story. Doesn't that help us? Where does Frown live?"

Rapunzel shakes her head. "I don't remember. I know it has a lot of rooms, though. For all the animals."

"The animals?" I ask.

Rapunzel nods. "Frau Gothel has *tons* of animals. And she

names them all after the stuff growing in her garden. Rosemary the monkey. Coriander the sheep. Nutmeg the tarantula. Sage the baby bear. Cinnamon the aardvark —"

Cinnamon? Seriously? "The aardvark's name is Cinnamon? Did Jonah tell you to say that?" I ask suspiciously.

She shakes her head. "His name is really Cinnamon."

"C-I-N-N-A-M-O-N. Cinnamon the aardvark." Jonah doubles over in laughter. "Hey, Abby, wanna try spelling aardvark?"

"No, I do not," I grumble.

"A-A-R-D-V-A-R-K," Rapunzel offers.

Show-off.

Jonah stands up straight and turns back to Rapunzel. "Did you get to live with all of the spice animals?" he asks her.

Rapunzel shakes her head. "Frau Gothel kept us all in separate rooms."

Shivers up my spine make me forget all about spelling. "So she collected animals?"

"She liked having pets," Rapunzel said.

I remember Frau Gothel referring to Rapunzel as a pet back in the tower. So creepy.

"Is that what she thought you were?" Jonah asks. "A pet?"

Rapunzel nods. "I guess so. I was the pet with really long hair."

"You're the pet who escaped," I say.

"She probably wouldn't care that I've escaped if she saw my hair now," Rapunzel says, running a hand through her bangs and looking hopeless.

"Your hair isn't the only thing that makes you special, Rapunzel," I say, meaning it. "You're sweet, you have a great singing voice, and you make up amazing lullabies. Plus, unlike me, you're a really good speller —"

"Oh!" Rapunzel cries. "That's it! Spellington Lane! I used to live on Spellington Lane!"

"Let's go!" Jonah cries.

"But, Jonah," I say, "we still don't know where it is or have any way to get there."

The mom in front of us, who'd been busy setting up her tent, turns around. "I can help! Please let me help. I'm sorry to have eavesdropped, but that is the saddest story I've ever heard. Please borrow my horse and carriage. It's not fancy, but it will take you where you want to go. It's the black-and-white one parked on the street. There's a map of the area inside. And bananas and onions. Take whatever you need. I'll even hold your spot for you if you want to come back."

Bananas and onions? Bananas I get, but onions? "Thank you," I say uncertainly.

She smiles. "You know what they say. An onion a day keeps the doctor at bay."

Jonah looks at me doubtfully. "People really say that? I'll have the bananas. You can have the onions."

The woman hugs her baby to her chest. "I can only imagine how sad your mother is — and your dad, too — and how much they miss you," she says to Rapunzel.

"Thank you!" we cry.

*"Ruff!"* Prince barks.

"No problem," the mom says, waving us off. "Good luck!"

"Can I drive?" Jonah asks as we start back toward the stone door. "Pretty, pretty please?"

"No way," I say.

"Why not?" he argues. "It's not like either of you has your license."

"Rapunzel's the oldest," I say. "She should drive. I'll navigate. I'm very good with maps."

"No problem," Rapunzel says.

We find the black-and-white carriage easily, and as the nice mom said, there is a map and a brown paper bag full of bananas and onions on the front seat. I study the map. It is surprisingly complex and detailed. There are roads and hills and villages and also lakes and waterfalls. The area where I think the tower is is marked FOREST. I guess that's why no one ever found Rapunzel.

Spellington Lane does not seem too far away. We'll get there in an hour, find Rapunzel her happy ending with her parents, swing back here to return the carriage, and then find our portal home. I bet it's somewhere at the palace. There were lots of shiny doors and surfaces to knock on, at least.

It'll take three hours, tops. In and out in one day. Yay, us!

"Let's go!" I call, claiming my seat.

We hit the road.

Uh-oh.

Rapunzel may be a great singer and speller, but she is not a great driver.

Neither Jonah nor I usually gets carsick, but after ten minutes, we are both very carriagesick. So is Prince. He's moaning and sticking his head out the window. I try to ignore the queasiness so I can study the map to direct Rapunzel which way to go, but it's not easy.

It gets worse as the sky gets darker. Once the sun has set entirely, I can barely read the map.

"I can't see the road," Rapunzel says.

"This carriage could really use headlights," Jonah says. "And the streets could use some streetlights."

"I could really use the light on my watch," I grumble. My trade may have been a little hasty.

"So what do we do?" Jonah asks.

Rapunzel points to the side of the road. "We might have to pull over and park for the night."

A wave of worry washes over me. There goes my three-hour plan.

After pulling over, we eat bananas and onions for dinner. Well, Jonah and I have bananas and onions, but Rapunzel and Prince have only bananas.

Jonah tries to give Prince a piece of his onion, but I swipe his hand away. "Onions are dangerous for dogs," I say. Obviously, I researched proper dog foods after we got Prince. That's my job as pet owner.

Hmm. Pet owner. I'm not sure I like being in the same category as Frau Gothel.

"You don't want an onion?" I ask Rapunzel.

She shakes her head. "I don't want my breath to be all stinky when I first meet my parents. I already have to worry about my hair."

I flinch. Right. Her horrible hair. Her messed-up mane. I'm kinda wishing she'd get over what we did to it already.

Jonah and I are too hungry to worry about bad breath. After dinner, we try to get cozy on the seats. At first, the horse disagrees with our plan to get some shut-eye, and keeps jerking us around. Finally, he stops, and the carriage is still.

"Shall I sing a lullaby?" Rapunzel offers.

"Yes, please," Jonah and I say.

I pull a baby blanket over my legs and place another one over Jonah. Then I cuddle Prince in my arms. Rapunzel clears her throat and I close my eyes.

*"Hello, moon; good night, sun.*
*Close your eyes, sweet little ones. . . ."*

I'm not awake for the rest.

# ✳ chapter eleven ✳

## This Is Not a Buffet

the next morning, I wake up to find Prince on my stomach and Jonah's foot in my nose.

Gross. At least he'd had the sense to take off his soccer cleats the night before. Talk about OUCH.

I sit up, moving Prince off my stomach. He lets out a snore, and Jonah wakes up, startled. I blink and gaze outside at the hazy morning light.

"How'd you sleep?" I ask Rapunzel, who is in the front seat, examining the ends of her hair with a sad look on her face.

She shakes her head. "I didn't."

"How come?"

"I don't know," she says. "I'm not used to sleeping outside. Or without a pillow."

"That didn't stop me," Jonah says.

Rapunzel yawns. "I need something to eat."

Jonah stretches his arms above his head. "Banana? Onion?"

She sighs. "Again?"

"That's all we have," I tell her.

"Frau might have kept me prisoner in her tower, but at least she was a good cook. All the food was really flavorful. She made great herb soups."

My stomach growls. I'd love some soup. Or really anything but a banana and an onion. But I eat one of each, as does Jonah. We need our strength for the day. Then Rapunzel starts driving again. It takes us about half an hour to get to Spellington Lane.

"How are we going to figure out which one is Rapunzel's parents' house?" Jonah asks as we turn onto the street.

"And how are we not going to get seen by Frau Gothel?" Rapunzel asks.

Oh, yeah. I forgot about the fact that Frau Gothel lives here, too. Even if she's not really a witch, she's still scary.

But as soon as we pull onto the dirt road, I realize we shouldn't have worried about finding the cottages. There are only two houses on Spellington Lane. One is a big cottage with a large garden that's surrounded by a blue fence. And then there is a smaller cottage that's slightly up the hill.

"The one on the hill must belong to your parents," I tell Rapunzel. "Because they can see down into the garden. That's how your mom saw the rapunzel."

"Yes, that big cottage is where Frau Gothel lives," Rapunzel says, nodding. "I remember it now. That's where I used to live until she moved me to the tower."

"You lived here for twelve years?" I ask.

She nods.

"And you never met your parents?"

She shakes her head.

I can't help but wonder why her parents never took her back if they lived so close by. I don't want to hurt her feelings by asking. What if they really *didn't* care about her? No. Impossible. They must not have known she was there. Or maybe Frau just wouldn't let them talk to her. They had made a deal after all. "I wonder why Frau Gothel moved you to the tower," I say instead.

"I don't know. She told me I'd be more comfortable without all the animals. They were getting big. Sage, the baby bear, thought my hair was a chew toy."

"Do you think we'll get to meet Cinnamon?" Jonah asks and then starts to add, "C-I-N-N-A—"

I roll my eyes. "Thanks, Jonah, I get it."

He snickers. "I want to meet the tarantula, too. Do you know tarantulas don't make spiderwebs? And if they lose one of their legs it grows back?"

"I do not want to meet a tarantula, thank you very much. And also, can you guys lower your voices? We don't want Frau — or the tarantula, or *Cinnamon* — to hear us."

"Oh, don't worry," Rapunzel says. "Sage sleeps until noon, and Frau doesn't let Nutmeg out of the house. But Cinnamon could be around."

Terrific. Good old Cinnamon.

"But anyway," she adds, "Frau isn't home."

"How do you know?" I ask.

Rapunzel peeks at the cottage. "Basil, her horse, isn't here. Maybe she's still at the tower. Or maybe she's riding around looking for me. Come on, let's stop in the garden. I can smell all the herbs and fruits from here. I used to eat them all the time when I was younger. Yum."

I hesitate. "I don't think that's a good idea. . . ."

Wasn't that how Rapunzel's dad got into this mess to begin with?

"For the first time in my life, I can make my own decisions," Rapunzel says, lifting her chin. "And I'm going to make them." With that, she hops out of the carriage and sneaks in through the blue-painted fence.

Jonah lunges after her.

"I don't think so," I say.

"I can make my own decisions, too," he says. "You're not my mother." His stomach growls loudly for emphasis.

"Jonah, when Mom isn't here, I'm in charge! Stay!"

He laughs. "I'm not a puppy. And you're not in charge." He follows behind Rapunzel.

Is it my imagination or is Jonah not taking me as seriously ever since I lost the spelling bee?

Prince runs after them, yapping loudly.

I don't even bother telling *him* to stay.

Obviously, I go, too.

The grass in the garden comes up to my ankles. It does smell good in here. Like fresh fruit, with a hint of spice and mint. There are plants everywhere and fruit hanging from trees.

Then I spot a weird-looking animal in a far-off corner of the garden. It looks a little like a pig but has high ears and a really long nose.

"Cinnamon! The aardvark!" Jonah calls out. Prince barks and starts toward the aardvark, but I grab my puppy and hold him tight. We do not need to attract any animal's attention. Especially one whose name I can't spell.

"Don't worry," Rapunzel says, munching on a berry. "Cinnamon is harmless. He won't bother us."

"I'm going to go over in a sec and say hello," Jonah says, his mouth full.

Wait a second. "JONAH!" I holler. "What's in your mouth? Are you eating a berry?"

"Huh?" he asks.

"Are you chewing on something?"

He shrugs. "I'm still hungry."

"Please tell me you are munching on a banana or an onion and not on something random from the garden."

109

He nods.

"Jonah, tell me the truth!"

He shakes his head. "Was that not a good idea?"

"No, it was not!" I'm so angry, I let Prince drop from my arms. "Is it at least what Rapunzel is eating?" I ask, nodding toward the red berries in Rapunzel's hand.

Jonah shakes his head again, looking guilty.

"Spit it out, spit it out!" I yell.

Jonah spits out what looks like a green leaf onto the ground. "Okay, okay. But Rapunzel said she ate stuff from here all the time!"

"But she probably knew what was safe and what wasn't! Do you know what's safe and what isn't?"

"No," he says sheepishly.

"Was that the only piece you ate?"

"No," he admits. "I tried a few things. . . ."

"This isn't a buffet!" I shriek.

I look down to catch Prince munching on something, too. I try to take it out of his mouth, but it's too late. Prince swallows whatever he was eating and lets out a satisfied bark. Great.

"I'm sorry!" Jonah is saying. "They tasted good!"

"Poison can taste good!" I argue.

"How do you know? Have you ever eaten poison?"

"Obviously not, Jonah. I'm here, aren't I?" Sometimes I can't help but wonder how we're even related. "Show me which ones you ate."

He points to three of the plants.

"Jonah, we've been here five minutes! How did you eat so much?"

"I was just nibbling," he grumbles.

One of them looks like a cherry, one looks like a blue grape, and one looks like a little green leaf.

"What do you think?" I ask Rapunzel.

"I don't know about the cherry or the blue grape, but that clover leaf is in my soup all the time. I'm sure you'll be fine," she tells Jonah, patting his shoulder.

"So nothing bad has ever happened after someone ate this stuff?" I press her.

She pales. "There was this one time, with Pepper the parrot."

"What happened to Pepper?" I ask, my heart pounding. "Did he die? Tell me he didn't die."

"He didn't die. He got really big."

"Big?" I swallow the lump in my throat.

"Yes, ginormous. He ate something from the garden and he grew. To my size."

"But, Rapunzel," I cry, "you said Frau never did any magic!"

"I didn't realize it was magic! I just thought it was a growth spurt or something. . . ." She bites her lip. "Does this mean Frau is a witch?"

"I think it's a definite possibility!" I say. "Maybe she gets her powers from the herbs!"

Rapunzel gasps. "But I left the tower! My teeth could have fallen out! My teeth could still fall out!"

"Maybe," I admit. "But she can't fly. She used a ladder to get up the tower. Maybe her herbs aren't all-powerful. Maybe she can only do some stuff. Like enlarge animals."

"I'd love to be your size," Jonah says to Rapunzel. "That would be so cool!"

"Jonah, if a bird became *my* size, then you would become the size of a house," Rapunzel explains to him.

"Even cooler!"

"Not cool!" I shout. "Where would you live? None of your clothes would fit! You'd be too big to sleep in your bed! What if you couldn't fit into the mirror or whatever takes you back to Smithville? What then?"

He blinks. "That's not so cool."

"No. Not so cool." I turn back to Rapunzel. "So what happened to the bird?"

"He shrank back to his original size eventually." She scrunches up her eyebrows. "I don't remember how."

"Now, don't eat anything else, Jonah," I warn. "Do you hear me? Nothing else!"

"Okay, okay," he says. "But I'm taking some of the blue grapes for the road."

"Can we go to my parents' house now?" Rapunzel asks before I can yell at Jonah again. "I'd like to meet them before my teeth fall out."

"You're the one who wanted to make a pit stop in the garden," I grumble.

Hurriedly, Rapunzel and I climb over the blue fence. Jonah follows me with Prince in his arms.

Silently, we march up the hill to Rapunzel's parents' house.

Rapunzel lifts her hand to knock on the door. Her arm is shaky. "Do I look okay?" she whispers, tugging on her hair again.

Her hair is even worse than before, now that she spent the night in a carriage.

"You look great," I lie. She needs all the confidence she can get.

"Do you think they'll recognize me?" she squeaks.

"You probably look pretty different than you did when you were a baby," Jonah says.

"Maybe you look like your mom when she was your age," I say. Everyone says I look like my mom when she was my age.

Rapunzel knocks twice on the door.

Prince barks.

No one answers.

"Um, Abby?" Jonah says.

"What, Jonah? We're kind of busy here."

"Prince is blue."

"Huh?"

"Should I knock again?" Rapunzel asks.

"Yes, of course. Jonah, what did you say?" I ask without looking at him.

"Prince. Is blue."

"Blue as in sad?" I ask.

Rapunzel knocks again. Prince barks again. Still no answer.

"No," Jonah says. "Blue as in the color blue."

I swivel my head to look at Prince.

Jonah's right.

My dog is no longer brown. He is now blue. I look at Jonah.

My brother is blue, too.

# ✳ chapter twelve ✳

## Knock, Knock

blue like the sky. Blue like the ocean. Blue like the poisoned blue grapes Jonah stole from Frau Gothel's garden.

I cannot believe that both my brother and my puppy are *blue*.

"Uh-oh," Jonah says, looking down at the blue skin of his hand. "This is bad, isn't it?"

I can only nod in shock.

"Should I knock again?" Rapunzel asks me nervously.

"Yes," I say, closing my eyes and pretending the blue doesn't exist. "Knock again."

She knocks one more time. Prince barks one more time.

I'm getting a bit of a headache.

"Who is it?" a female voice finally asks.

Good. At least not everything is going wrong. First I'll reunite Rapunzel with her parents. Then I'll worry about turning Jonah and Prince back to their regular colors.

"It's Rapunzel," Rapunzel says nervously.

"Rapunzel who?" the woman asks.

"Rapunzel, your daughter," she says.

"I don't have a daughter," the woman snaps.

I step up to the door, getting nervous. "Your husband gave her away when she was born," I explain. "He traded her for the herb rapunzel. Now she's all grown up and she escaped and she's so excited to meet you!"

The woman cracks open the door. I can see the glow of her light brown eyes peering out from the shadows. Her eyes then dart down toward Prince, who is cowering near my ankle.

"I don't like dogs," the woman says. "Especially blue ones."

"Hey!" Jonah pipes up. "It's not easy being blue!"

"And I don't have a daughter," the woman adds firmly.

"But I . . ." Rapunzel's eyes fill with tears. "Don't you remember me?"

"I'm sorry, but I have no idea what you're talking about. You should leave and take your strange friends with you." The woman slams the door shut.

Rapunzel takes a step back, like she's been slapped.

I feel like I've been slapped, too. I can't believe that just happened. Rapunzel's mother doesn't even remember her. How could a mother forget about her own kid?

"She doesn't want me," Rapunzel whispers, and buries her face in her hands.

"It's her loss," I say, desperate to make her feel better. I put my arm around Rapunzel, feeling guilty. It was my idea to come here. Now Rapunzel is rejected by her mother, and Jonah and Prince are blue.

"We don't need her," I add quickly. "We'll go back to the castle! We still have our spot in the line. We'll meet Pickles. That can be your happy ending! Who needs parents? Not you!"

I hold my breath, hoping she cheers up.

Rapunzel can only shake her head and let out a small sob.

"Okay, forget about the prince. That's all right. You barely know him. What about your songs? You can become a famous singer! You'll give concerts! You'll be amazing!" I sound slightly hysterical. Maybe because I am. First Jonah and I destroyed Rapunzel's hair, then I broke her heart. We definitely messed up this story.

Rapunzel ignores me. She spins around and runs.

"Rapunzel, wait!" I yell, chasing after her.

Blue Jonah follows right behind me. Blue Prince chases us both.

Rapunzel sprints to the carriage and jumps onto the front seat, grabbing the reins. "I should never have listened to you." Her eyes are red, and her nose is running.

"I admit we made a few mistakes. . . ." I say.

"You were wrong about everything! I'm going to the one place I feel safe!"

"Where?" I ask. "The palace?"

"No! I'm going back to the place that has my books and my poems and my pillow and my instruments and my conditioner! You guys ruined everything! My hair and my life! I'm going back to the tower!"

She takes off, leaving us stranded at the side of the road.

Immediately, we hear the sound of hooves approaching from the other direction. Slowly, I turn around. A horse is approaching. An old woman is on the horse. An old woman in black overalls and black rubber boots.

Crumbs. My heart races. It's Frau and Basil, and they're headed right toward us.

# * chapter thirteen *

## My Brother the Chameleon

hide!" I yell.

"Where?" Jonah asks.

"Behind a tree?"

"There are no trees!"

My eyes land on the blue fence. "There!"

I grab my blue brother, hide behind him, and pull both of us against the fence. "Stay still. Pretend you're the fence. Blend in. Don't even breathe."

"But my sweatshirt is yellow!"

"Take it off!"

He takes it off and shoves it behind him. Luckily, he's wearing blue jeans.

"Pick up Prince!" I order as I try to hide behind my brother's scrawny little blue body. Jonah does as he's told.

"Prince," I whisper into my dog's floppy ear. "If you stay quiet, I will let you eat an entire jar of peanut butter when we get home. No — five entire jars!"

Prince wriggles in Jonah's arms, but he hides his pink tongue inside his mouth.

We freeze.

Frau Gothel dismounts from the horse. This is the first time I've gotten a full look at her. Her hair is a dull green — like the color of weeds. She wears it in a high ponytail. Talk about having a bad hair day.

She's holding a brown paper bag stuffed with . . . I have no idea.

"Where could that girl be?" Frau mutters aloud, looking angry. "Basil, we'll search again in a few hours. I need to eat some lunch and feed the other animals and see what I can do with all this hair."

Oh! The bag is filled with Rapunzel's hair! But what could she do with it? Is she going to make a potion with it?

Frau Gothel disappears inside the house. Jonah, Prince, and I don't move a muscle until we hear the door close. For the first time, I'm glad Jonah is blue. Otherwise we would have been caught for sure.

I heave an uneasy sigh of relief and toss Jonah his hoodie. "Let's go."

"Where? Home?" he asks hopefully.

"Not yet," I say. "We have to talk some sense into Rapunzel. We have to go back to the tower."

"How do we get there?" he asks. "Rapunzel took our ride."

"We walk. At least we won't get carriagesick."

So we walk. Jonah and I drag our heels, and even Prince mopes along. We get stared at by people passing by in carriages or on horseback. Of course we do. My brother and our dog are blue.

"You look like a Smurf," I tell Jonah.

"I know." He sighs. "I should have listened to you. I shouldn't have said you weren't my mom. I guess you are in charge when we're here. Kind of. S-O-R-Y?"

"S-O-R-R-Y," I tell him. "I'm sorry you're blue. But I forgive you. You're exonerated. E-X-O-N-A . . . never mind. I have no idea how to spell that." I sigh, too. "I am a bad speller."

"You are not a bad speller, Abby. You're going to have to get over not winning."

It's not that easy. "Some things are hard for a little brother to understand. Let's just walk."

After a long while, we arrive at the tower. We peer up at the window, and I can make out Rapunzel just inside, her back to us. Of course, there's no hair to hang out the window now.

"Rapunzel!" I yell up. "Rapunzel, come down through the trapdoor! I'm sorry it didn't work out with your parents! But you can't stay here. We'll go back to the palace. We'll meet Pickles!"

No response.

"I can see you in the window!" I holler.

She turns around quickly and closes the shutters.

Now, where is that secret door? All I see is beige stone.

"Stay right here," I tell Jonah and Prince. "Holler if you see Frau." I don't know about Prince, but at least now I know Jonah will listen to me.

It takes me ten minutes, but I eventually find the hidden door by running my fingers along the side of the tower until I hit a crack. Then I drag my fingernails along the crack and tug. I also get a bunch of thorn scratches on my hands in the process. Good thing I'm wearing long sleeves. Ouch.

When I finally pull open the secret door, I climb up the winding stairs. The trapdoor is locked tight. I knock.

"Rapunzel! Let me in!" I holler.

"Go away," she says.

"Come on, Rapunzel! Please unlock the door!"

"No! I'm never leaving again. I'm safe in here."

I sigh. I don't want to leave Jonah and Prince alone for too long outside, so I make my way back outside the tower. My brother is studying his blue hands. The puppy is chasing his blue tail.

"We're not going anywhere, Rapunzel!" I call up. "We want you to come out!"

She opens the shutters. "I am never leaving again. I hate it outside."

"Rapunzel, come on. The witch is probably really mad at you. She could do something awful. Magical awful! With her herbs. You have to get out of there!"

"What are we supposed to do?" Jonah mutters.

"I don't know," I admit. "We need to coax her out. What would get *you* to come out?"

"Oh, Rapunzel!" Jonah calls up. "If you come out, you can have French fries and ketchup!"

"We don't have French fries and ketchup," I tell him.

"No kidding. If we did, I would have eaten them. You asked me what would get me out, and that's what would. I don't think onions and bananas are going to work."

"Jonah, we really have to get her out before Frau comes back," I say worriedly. Things are not looking good. Not only is Rapunzel not cooperating, but Jonah and Prince are still blue, and I have *no* idea what time it is in Smithville, or how we will get back —

Jonah jumps on the balls of his feet. "I know, I know! Instead of trying to bribe Rapunzel with fun stuff, we should annoy her until she comes out!"

"How?"

He clears his throat.

*"I know a song that gets on everybody's nerves, everybody's nerves, everybody's nerves. I know a song that gets on everybody's nerves, and this is how it goes: I know a song that gets on everybody's nerves —"*

I join in. What choice do I have?

We sing. And sing some more.

*"I know a song that gets on everybody's nerves!"*

A book flies by my head and lands with a thud beside me. "You guys are driving me crazy!" Rapunzel yells.

"It's working!" Jonah says gleefully. "Keep going! Louder!"

*Badoom, badoom!*

I think I hear something.

Jonah keeps singing. *"I know a song that gets on everybody's nerves! Everybody's —"*

"Jonah, shush! Listen!"

*Badoom, badoom, badoom, badoom.*

"Somebody's coming!" Jonah says, his blue face paling. "Do you think it's Frown?"

"Who else could it be?" I answer. "We have to take cover!"

I grab Prince, and we all duck behind the closest tree.

*Badoom, badoom, badoom!*

I peek out in fear. There is a horse approaching. But wait. Basil is brown. This horse is white. It's *not* the wannabe witch.

There's a young man on the horse. He's wearing glittery robes, and he's staring in shock at the tower.

Who could it be?

# ✳ chapter fourteen ✳

## Pickles Charming

Oh! I jump in my spot. "It's him! It's him! It's the prince!"

*Ruff, ruff!*"

"Pickles! I mean Pickles," I say. "This is what happened in the story! Pickles rides by and sees Rapunzel. Oh, yay! Maybe *he* can cheer her up. Maybe her happy ending will be the original one after all!"

"I thought you said he hears Rapunzel sing?" Jonah asks.

"That is what's supposed to happen," I say, putting down Prince. But Rapunzel isn't singing. She's too sad to sing. She hasn't sung a word all day. So why did the prince stop?

I step out from behind the tree. "Hello there!" I say to the prince.

He's wearing a gold crown and has round, rosy cheeks, a button nose, and short, messy brown hair. He looks like he's about Rapunzel's age.

"Hello," Pickles says. "I heard someone singing. Was that you?"

A lightbulb turns on in my head. "That *was* me! And my brother. We were singing! *That's* why you stopped. You heard *us*!"

He nods, looking confused. "Yes. That's what I said."

"That is so cool!" Jonah exclaims, and jumps out from behind the tree.

The prince stares at Jonah. "You're blue!"

"Yes," I agree. "He is."

Prince darts out from behind the tree, too.

"And so is your dog."

"Yes," I say. "They are both blue. And you're Pickles."

He looks confused. "I'm what?"

"Pickles. Every time we say Prince —"

*"Ruff, ruff!"*

129

"Our dog barks. His name is Prince, too."

"Ah," Pickles says. "I get it. Okay, then. Well, my real name is Prince Tristan. But you can call me Pickles if you'd like."

Pickles jumps off his horse and bends down to pat Prince's back. *Our* Prince wags his tail.

Pickles is shorter than most of the other princes I've seen in fairy tales, but there's something very kind about him.

"We're so glad you're here," I tell him. "We need —"

He sighs and massages his forehead. "Diamonds? Sapphires? Rubies? I don't have any on me. I'm sorry. I just left the palace for a short ride on my lunch break. If you come by the palace and wait in line, I'll be happy to consider your request. I hand out lots and lots of gems. That's all I do! All day!"

He's about to climb back onto his horse.

"Don't go! I just need you to listen to something!" I say.

"You can tell me your whole story tomorrow. I have a lot of sapphires to give away."

"No, no, you don't understand. We don't want any sapphires!"

He pulls on his horse's reins. "We have rubies, too."

"WE DON'T WANT ANY GEMS!" Jonah yells. "WE

JUST NEED YOU TO LISTEN TO OUR FRIEND SING. COME WITH US! YOU HAVE TO! I'M BLUE."

Pickles — I mean Prince Tristan — stops moving and stares at us.

"Please come listen to Rapunzel sing," I say, more calmly. "She has a beautiful voice. She makes up her own songs and everything."

The prince reconsiders. "You don't need rubies?"

"We don't," I promise.

"All right. I'll listen. I love music. I actually play the flute. When I have time, that is. Interesting song you were singing before. It was very catchy."

Jonah claps and then belts out, *I know a song that gets on everybody's —*"

"Don't, Jonah. We don't want to scare him away." I turn back to the tower and call up to the window. "Rapunzel! Rapunzel, we need you to sing."

The shutters stay closed.

"Rapunzel!" I call again. "Pickles is here! He wants to hear you sing. Come on. I know you can do it! You sang for the baby!"

Silence.

"Please sing, Rapunzel!" Jonah yells.

Prince howls up at the window, as if trying to plead with Rapunzel, too.

Silence.

"Do you want to come down instead?" I yell. "Pickles wants to meet you!"

"I think I better go," the prince says. "Sorry, guys, but it doesn't look like anything is happening here, and I only take an hour off. . . ."

My brother and I look at each other helplessly.

"Nice to meet you," the prince says. "Good luck!"

"Wait!" Jonah calls out.

The prince stops. "Yes?"

"Um, how come you only get an hour off? Aren't you the prince? Can't you leave the palace whenever you want?"

"I'm too busy during the day," the prince explains. "There are so many poor people in the kingdom. And it's my responsibility to help them. It's the right thing to do and it's my dad's dying wish."

"I'm so sorry about your father," I say. "But that's really nice of him to want to give away all those gems."

"It is. And I enjoy helping people. But . . ." Prince Tristan's voice trails off.

"But what?"

"But I'm stuck inside all day. I hate being stuck inside. I like to ride my horse! I like to explore! I know I shouldn't complain. There are worse places to be stuck in all day than a palace made of jewels. But I'm stuck there. Forever. And after my father dies, I'll have to be king because I'm the oldest. They even have my wife picked out for me. Her name is Grumpen. She was groomed to be queen. Isn't that the most unmusical name you've ever heard?"

From the corner of my eye, I see a flash of jagged hair in the tower window. Is Rapunzel listening to this? I hope she's listening. Maybe she'll like what she hears and come down?

"Do you have your flute here?" I ask Prince Tristan, getting an idea.

He nods. "I like to practice in the woods."

"Play us something!" I suggest. Who knows — maybe we'll reverse the story. Rapunzel might hear *his* music and fall in love with him!

"You sure?" he asks.

Jonah and I nod enthusiastically. Prince barks.

Pickles removes the flute from his bag and begins to play.

*La, la, LA, lalalalala, LA, lala . . .*

Hey! He's good. Really good.

The song he's playing sounds fun and upbeat. He plays for a few minutes and seems like he's winding down, when a melodic voice from above suddenly joins in.

*"A beautiful day,*
*A glittering sky,*
*The sun full and bright,*
*If only I could fly."*

It's Rapunzel! She's singing with him!

I glance up and see her peeking out the window, singing along.

The prince looks up and smiles and keeps playing his flute.

They are playing together! And they sound pretty great. By the time they finish the song, Jonah and I are grinning.

"You have a beautiful voice," Prince Tristan calls up, squinting into the sunlight.

"Thank you. You play the flute very well," Rapunzel replies bashfully.

The prince motions to us while still gazing up toward the window. "Are you the lady that the girl and blue boy wanted me to meet?"

"Yes!" I squeal. "That's her. Doesn't she have a wonderful voice? And she even makes her own musical instruments!"

"Wow," Prince Tristan says, blinking. "Hi there. I can't really see you. Can you come down? Or I can come up? I would like to meet the lady who sings like an angel, writes her own songs, and makes her own instruments."

Woo-hoo! It worked! Rapunzel and the prince are going to fall in love, and this story will end happily after all! Grumpen who?

"No," Rapunzel suddenly says. She slams the shutters closed.

What? Why "no"? "Rapunzel, what's wrong?" I ask. "Pickles — Tristan — wants to come up and meet you."

"He can't," she says.

"Why not?"

"Because . . . because . . . I'm too ugly for anyone to see!"

"I'm sure you're not ugly," the prince says.

"I *am*," she insists. "At least my hair is. I used to be the girl with long, gorgeous hair and now I'm just . . . nothing."

I can't believe she's still obsessing about her hair. At some point, she's going to have to let it go and get on with her life.

I suddenly experience a pang of recognition.

Isn't that what Jonah just said to me about the spelling bee?

My face heats up as something clicks in my mind. *Ohhhhhh.*

"But, Rapunzel," Prince Tristan says, "I don't care what you look like. I love your voice and your words."

"I'm sorry," Rapunzel says. "I'm just not special enough for you. Even my parents didn't want me. They gave me up when I was a baby. You wouldn't want me, either."

Her words squeeze my heart. She thinks she's unlovable. "What happened with your parents had nothing to do with you!" I call up. "You weren't even born when they gave you up! And you *are* special."

"If your parents didn't want you, they're fools," the prince calls up. "I think you're amazing. Who are they, anyway?"

"I don't even know their names," Rapunzel responds from behind the closed shutters. "All I know is that they live on

136

Spellington Lane. I went by today to meet them, and my mom said she didn't have a daughter. She denied my existence."

Prince Tristan shakes his head. "Hold your horses. Your parents live on Spellington Lane? Next to Frau Gothel? I know your parents!"

Rapunzel gasps. "How do you know my parents?"

"They came to see me! Your parents have been looking for you for years. They are searching the world for you as we speak. I don't know where they are, but I know they love you and are trying to find you."

The shutters fly open and Rapunzel looks down at us. "But . . . then who are the people we saw at their house?"

"Your parents rented out their house!" Prince Tristan explains.

Huh?

"Fifteen years ago, right after your parents made the deal with Frau Gothel, they begged her to reconsider. She said she would give you back if they gave her two hundred rubies."

"Two hundred rubies?" I exclaim. "That's a lot of rubies."

As I speak, I notice that there are light, little threads crisscrossing over my sneaker. What is that? Oh, probably strands of

Rapunzel's hair. I bet I'll be finding pieces of hair everywhere for the next few days.

"That is a lot of rubies indeed," the prince goes on, while Rapunzel leans out the window, listening intently. "They tried to earn the gems from villagers by cooking and cleaning. Meanwhile, they watched you grow, Rapunzel. They used to sit on their roof and watch you play in the garden or with the animals. Three years ago, when my father decided to start giving away gems to whoever needed them, your parents were the first ones to come see me. They had already saved up a hundred rubies and begged me to give them a hundred more. Of course I did. I was only thirteen and I felt so bad for them. And for you. But when your parents brought the rubies to Frau Gothel's house to make the trade, Frau told them you had run away."

Rapunzel's jaw drops. "Run away? I didn't! Frau locked me in this tower!"

"But your parents didn't know that," the prince explains. "Frau Gothel probably moved you to the tower after they came to get you. They believed her, too. They felt so guilty. They decided to use the rubies to go travel and try to find you. To bring you home."

"My ankle itches," Jonah complains. Prince lets out a frantic-sounding bark.

"Shhh," I tell Jonah. "You're ruining the moment."

Rapunzel gazes down at the prince, her cheeks flushed. "So Frau Gothel lied to my parents?"

"Yes."

"And now they're looking for me?"

"Yes."

"So they don't hate me?"

"Of course they don't hate you! You're their daughter! They're trying to find you!"

Rapunzel gasps. At first I think it's from happiness, but then she yells, "Look out behind you! It's Nutmeg!"

"It's what?" asks the prince.

I spin around.

It's Nutmeg the giant tarantula. He's the size of a bicycle and has what seems like a million long, very hairy legs.

And he's inching toward us.

# * chapter fifteen *

## Nobody Likes Spiders

Oh no oh no oh no. My heart freezes. My whole body freezes.

I look down at my feet. The tangle of threads twining itself around my sneakers? Not Rapunzel's hair.

It's a spiderweb.

*That's* why Jonah said his ankle was itchy. And why Prince is barking frantically.

While we were listening to Prince Tristan's story, the elephant-sized spider was stealthily wrapping us in a web. And we hadn't even noticed.

Now our feet — and Prince's paws —are glued to the ground. We're trapped. Totally trapped.

I hear cackling to the right. I turn my head and spot Frau Gothel looming ominously beside us.

"But tarantulas can't spin webs!" Jonah says.

More cackling. "I taught mine to," Frau Gothel says. "I'm an excellent trainer."

Of course *she* is.

"Who is that?" Prince Tristan asks us, frowning at Frau.

"The wannabe witch," Jonah replies.

"I'm not a wannabe," Frau Gothel says. "I'm also not a witch. I am a sorceress. I grow herbs that can do magical things. I turned you blue, didn't I?" she says to Jonah.

"Yes. And I could really use a reversal herb," Jonah says. "If you don't mind."

"I don't think it will make a difference," Frau Gothel says. "Once Nutmeg eats you."

I feel a dart of fear. Another spiderweb wraps around my leg. *Ahhh!*

I swallow, hard. I kick my foot, trying to escape, but it just makes the web tangle more tightly around my ankle.

"Abby," Jonah says. His voice is small and scared. "I'm stuck. This stuff feels like stretched-out bubble gum!"

"This is not exactly how I planned to spend my time off," cracks Prince Tristan.

Frau Gothel cackles again. She whips her scary weed ponytail from side to side. "I trapped you all! Hahaha! I knew Rapunzel was being coached by someone. I didn't expect it was the three of you, but no matter. How dare you try to get Rapunzel, my favorite pet, to escape? And you, Prince Tristan! You think you're so powerful with your rubies and your emeralds. How will they help you here? They won't! They're useless against my herbs. My Nutmeg will get you all. He's been eating strength berries to make his web extra strong!"

Nutmeg and his eight striped, orange-and-black hairy legs are crawling directly toward me. His eyes look like marbles. I hold my breath. My heart is beating a hundred times a minute.

"I'm coming to help!" Rapunzel yells down.

"Oh, no, you're not," Frau Gothel says. "I'm coming to stop you!" She runs over to the tower's base and disappears inside the hidden door.

Prince Tristan drops to his knees and tries to tear the web apart with his hands. "It won't rip!" he cries.

I have an idea. "Jonah — use your cleats!"

"Right! My cleats!" My brother starts kicking the web, but trips instead.

"No, Jonah, take the cleat off," I order. "Pretend the web is . . . hair."

My brother takes off his shoe and smashes it against the web. "It's not working! These stupid shoes are good for nothing. Well, except playing soccer, probably."

Frau comes back outside. "She may have locked the hatch, but I'm locking her in the tower." She reaches into a black leather purse and pulls out a bar. Then she barricades the hidden door with it.

We're trapped. We're *really* trapped. I am dizzy with fear.

Nutmeg takes a few more steps toward me. He opens his mouth. . . .

Rapunzel leans over the window ledge. "Nutmeg, are you tired? Remember how I used to sing you to sleep? *Hello, moon; good night, sun; close your eyes, little one.*"

Is Nutmeg yawning? I think he is!

"It's working!" I call up softly. "Keep singing the lullaby!"

Rapunzel keeps going. *"Tomorrow will be another day, then we'll have time to play."*

Nutmeg stretches his many legs and lies down on his belly.

"Absolutely not, Nutmeg. Wake up," Frau yells. "It's not even dark out! It's the middle of the day!" She tries to walk toward him but gets blocked by the web.

Rapunzel sings on, in a soft, drowsy voice. *"Rest that head on a leg, and don't eat my friends, I beg."*

Nutmeg closes his eyes. Then opens them again.

Prince somehow maneuvers his way through the sticky spiderweb to investigate, his tail wagging. His little nose sniffs at Nutmeg's scary spider fangs. He yips and wags his tail again until his whole dog-butt shakes from side to side.

Rapunzel: *"Little Nutmeg, you're very cute but also creepy, and now you are very sleepy."*

Nutmeg is snoring. He is officially asleep.

We're safe! Yahoo! I give Rapunzel two thumbs up.

Meanwhile, Jonah is still hammering away at the web. The cleats seem to be working. "My soccer shoes are doing the trick. I just have to hit harder. Here, take one, Pickles!" He throws his left shoe to the prince, who's ensnared beside him.

Stepping back from the spiderweb, Frau twists her green ponytail around one finger. "You think you can sing some lullaby

144

and we're done? I don't think so. I may not be able to fly or make your teeth fall out, but turning animals giant and people blue aren't the only things my special plants can do!" She reaches into her purse and pulls out what looks like a bag of leaves. She shoves the entire handful into her mouth, gobbling them up. "I have to thank you guys for cutting Rapunzel's hair. I've been experimenting on my pets with herbs for years, but I never thought to use *their* hair or venom or whiskers in my brews until today! So thank you! Wait until you see what this special salad can do! Watch me now!"

"That's disgusting," Jonah says, making a face. "Not even ketchup would make that taste good."

At first, Frau starts to tremble. Then she starts to change. Her legs stretch out into scary spider arms. Spider arms with bear claws. And her nose stretches into . . . an aardvark's nose? *Cinnoman*'s nose! I mean, *Cinoman*! I mean . . . UCH. Who cares? However it's spelled, Frau Gothel is now one giant freaky-looking animal. She still has her high green ponytail. And she's heading right toward Jonah.

"I will get you!" yells the hybrid animal in a chillingly human voice. "I will tear you apart with my arms and eat you!"

"Leave my brother alone!" I yell, aching to protect him. But I can't move. I'm still pinned in the spiderweb.

Meanwhile, Prince Tristan keeps scraping the cleat against the web.

"Noooo!" We hear the cry from above. Rapunzel is climbing out the window. "I'm coming!"

"Don't jump!" I yell. "You're too high! You'll get hurt!"

But she doesn't listen. She jumps straight out the window. "Wheeee!" she yells as she flies down. She lands on the Frau-Monster, knocking her down, and then bounces into the thorns by the tower as though Frau were a trampoline.

The Frau-Monster groans in pain but tries to stand back up.

As Prince Tristan frees himself from the web, Prince — the dog — escapes with the end of the spiderweb in his mouth. He jumps over the Frau-Monster and dashes around again and again and again, until the Frau-Monster is all tied up.

The sorceress groans in frustration, wriggling about help-lessly in her own web.

"Good job, Prince Junior!" Prince Tristan says.

"Rapunzel?" I ask nervously, spying her lying facedown in the thorns. "Are you all right?"

She slowly stands up. Her hands are shaking. "I can't . . . I can't . . ."

"You can't believe you jumped out of a tower? Me neither!" Jonah cries, finally chopping himself free. "Good job!"

She touches the sides of her face with her hands. "I can't . . . I can't . . ."

"You can't what?" Prince Tristan asks. "Are you hurt?"

"I can't see," she says finally. "I can't see you, or Abby, or Jonah, or anyone. I can't see anything. I've lost my sight."

Dread fills my stomach.

"Don't worry," Jonah says. "That happened to the prince —"

*"Ruff, ruff!"*

"— in the original story, and he ended up fine! He got his sight back. You're going to be okay."

My heart sinks. "But, Jonah, Rapunzel's the one with the magical tears. She's the one who fixed the prince's eyes."

"Well, maybe if she cries, her eyes will fix themselves!"

"I *am* crying," Rapunzel says as tears run down her cheeks. "And I still can't see."

Oh, no. This is all our fault. We should never have gone through the mirror. We should never have climbed up Rapunzel's hair. This time we *really* ruined everything.

# ✳ chapter sixteen ✳

## The Tears

Prince Tristan tosses me the cleat and runs toward Rapunzel. He puts his arm around her and leads her to sit down by a tree.

As soon as I manage to free myself, I join them.

"I'm so sorry," I tell Rapunzel. "We'll fix this. We'll figure out a way."

She sighs. "I can't believe I wasted so much time worrying about my hair. When now I can't see! It really puts the other stuff into perspective."

"That is so true," I say.

"This doesn't change how I feel," Prince Tristan murmurs. "Rapunzel, I love you."

"You love me?" she repeats. "Are you sure?"

He murmurs yes and kisses both her hands.

I turn away to give them a moment of privacy. Hey, where did Jonah go? I look around and spot him in the carriage, rummaging in the food bag. How can he be hungry at a time like this?

He finds what he's looking for and comes running back toward us. He's peeling an onion. And crying. And smiling.

What in the world is he doing?

"I have an idea!" he says. As the tears roll down his cheeks, he stands right above Rapunzel. One of his tears lands right on her forehead and slowly rolls down into her eye. Another one goes into the other eye.

I'm too confused to tell him to stop.

Then the craziest thing happens. Rapunzel blinks. And blinks again. She jumps up and throws her arms around Jonah. "I can see! My eyes are healed!"

"My tears were magic," Jonah says. "I knew it!"

Huh? "But why?" I wonder. "I thought Rapunzel's tears were the ones that were magic. . . ."

Jonah is beaming. "They were probably magic because of all the herbs the sorceress put in her soup. And since I ate all that stuff in the garden, I thought maybe I had magic tears, too."

We hear the Frau-Monster groan, but she's barely struggling anymore. She seems to be giving up.

"I guess you did," I say. "Good thinking, Jonah! Now, what should we do with Frau Gothel?" I wonder out loud.

"We should lock her in the tower. That would be a good revenge," Jonah says.

"We have a special tower for people like her," Prince Tristan says. "It's called jail."

"Can you at least turn me back into my normal self first?" Frau Gothel grumbles. "There are reversal herbs in my purse." She nods toward her black purse that's now sitting beside a tree. "The one I need is purple and looks like a sunflower."

"She'll definitely be easier to move around as a human," Prince Tristan says.

"Get me some reversal herbs, too!" Jonah says. "Although how cool would it be if I went to school blue?"

"Not cool," I inform him. I hurry over to the purse. It's overflowing with stuff, so I empty its contents on the ground. There are yellow and green seeds and some green plants. I see one that looks like purple sunflowers, but I hesitate. "How do we know she's not lying? What if the purple sunflowers turn her into an even more giant Frau-Monster?"

Prince dashes up behind me. He sniffs the herbs and next thing I know, he scarfs down a mouthful of the yellow-green seeds.

"Oh, no, Prince!" I cry. "What did you do?" I wait for something horrible to happen. But instead, as I watch, the blue drains from his fur. Almost instantly, he is back to his regular brown color. "Way to go, Prince!" I cheer, relieved. Prince may not be the world's best listener, but he might still be a genius.

Also, I'm glad he really likes pumpkin seeds. And things that look like pumpkin seeds.

"Thanks a lot, stupid dog," Frau says, her tone snide. "Too bad you're not one of my pets. I'd know what to do with you."

Prince growls in her face.

Now that I know for sure that the yellow-green seeds are the reversal ones, I hand some to Jonah and some to the Frau-Monster.

Jonah quickly swallows the seeds and returns to his normal color. The Frau-Monster does the same and turns back into a Frau-person.

Prince Tristan adjusts the spiderweb so that it accommodates Frau's new shape. "I'll take her to the castle jail."

"Wait," I say, realizing something: Jonah and I still need to find a way back to Smithville, and in our last fairy tale, we had to have a fairy create a portal for us. Frau Gothel isn't a fairy, but she can obviously do magical things. "Frau Gothel?" I ask. "Could you make a portal home for us?"

She snorts. "You expect me to help you? After everything you did to ruin my life?"

I dig my shoe into the ground, avoiding her eyes. "Is that a no?"

"I think you should reconsider," Prince Tristan tells Frau sternly. "I might be willing to give you a lighter sentence if you cooperate."

"Can I bring one of my animals to jail?" she asks.

"Which one?" Prince Tristan asks.

She smiles. "Nutmeg?"

"The giant spider? No. Maybe a small bird or a dog."

Prince hides behind my leg.

Prince Tristan scratches Prince behind the ears. "Not this dog. Help them get home, and then we'll pick something."

Frau swings her weedy ponytail from side to side. "What are you looking for exactly?"

"Something shimmery?" I say. "Usually, we knock on it a few times, and it takes us home. We used a witch's cauldron once."

She licks her lips. "Hmm. My herbs are magical, not me. You should go back to my garden and knock on the soil. There's a lot of magic in there."

The garden! Where the story of Rapunzel began.

The prince lifts Frau Gothel up and places her on his horse.

"You can take her horse," he tells us. "And leave it at her house," he adds. "But before I go. Rapunzel?"

"Yes?" she asks hopefully.

"I really do love you. That wasn't just something I said to make you feel better before. Come with me. We'll bring Frau

Gothel to jail, and then, after that, we can be together. We could get married. You'll move into my palace with me."

She hesitates. "But —"

"You can help me give out the gems. We'll do it together! We'll live and work in the palace!"

Rapunzel looks back at the tower and then at the prince. "No."

The prince's face falls. "No, you don't love me? Is it because I'm short? Do you not want to marry me?"

She quickly shakes her head. "Oh, no, I do love you. I think you're the perfect height. I think you're sweet and adorable and brave. I meant, no, I don't want to hide away in your castle. I'm tired of being locked up. I want to explore! I want to find my parents! Will you search the world with me to find them?"

The prince beams and pulls Rapunzel into a hug. "Of course I will. It can be a traveling honeymoon/search party!"

"But what about your duties as prince?" I ask, thinking of the kind mom with her baby daughter we met in line. "Don't you have to stay home and give away gems to people? What about Grumpen? Aren't you supposed to marry her? Aren't you supposed to be king?"

The prince grows serious. "Today I realized something. I don't want to be king. Being king is a lot like being locked in a tower. My brother can marry Grumpen. My brother can be King Tristan the Sixth! Well, he can't be King Tristan, since his name is Bartholomew, but he can be King Bartholomew the *First*. I want to travel the world with Rapunzel and help her find her parents. And I could still give out gems when I travel. But maybe instead of just handing out gems, I could teach the people to mine themselves. There are still a lot of sapphires and emeralds in the mountains."

"That would be fantastic," Rapunzel says. "We could teach the people to plant, too! I learned a lot when I lived at Frau Gothel's. We'll teach them to grow their own food! Nonmagical food, preferably." She hesitates. "There is one more thing, though. . . ."

"What? Anything for you, my love."

"Abby told me that some people have concerts. They sing. I was wondering if you wanted to do something like that. I could sing my songs, and you could play the flute. We could make music for people all over the kingdom. Wouldn't that be wonderful? What do you think?"

"I love it," the prince says with a laugh. "We'll start a band. We'll leave tonight."

"First, you just need to return the carriage we borrowed to the nice lady with the baby. She really helped us," I chime in.

"Of course," says the prince. "We'll give her enough gems to take her baby to college!"

"You guys have college here?" I ask.

"Definitely," Prince Tristan says. "College is the name of a mountain resort by the lake."

Ah.

"So what are you going to call your band?" Jonah asks Rapunzel.

The prince smiles. "How about Pickles and Rapunzel?"

We all agree it's a great name.

Rapunzel wraps me in a hug. "Thank you for everything. I'm so glad I let you into the tower."

"Me too," I tell her.

She looks into my eyes. "If it wasn't for you, I would never have known the truth."

"What truth?"

She stands up straight. "That I am not just my hair."

I hug her hard. Rapunzel might not realize it, but she's taught me something, too. "Good luck," I tell her.

Jonah and I wave good-bye as Prince Tristan and Rapunzel climb into the black-and-white carriage. They drive off, with Prince Tristan's horse dutifully carrying Frau Gothel behind them.

Jonah and I ride Basil back to Spellington Lane. Jonah sits behind me and keeps his (happily nonblue) arms around my waist while Prince trots along beside us.

When we get back to Frau Gothel's house, we climb off the horse and slip back through the blue gate into the garden.

"You sure we shouldn't take some samples?" Jonah asks me, looking around at all the herbs and fruits.

"No samples," I say firmly.

He smirks. "What about Cinnamon? Want to bring him to school for a spelling bee show-and-tell?"

"Ha, ha, ha. Definitely not. We're not bringing home any more pets, anyway. Do you want to do the knocking?"

"Sure," Jonah says. He crouches down on his knees. He

knocks on the ground once. Twice. Three times. The soil starts to swirl. Whoa. It's like a muddy whirlpool.

"Here we go," I say.

Prince backs away.

Oh, no.

"Not again," Jonah says, biting his lip. "Come on, Prince!"

Prince growls, and takes another step back.

No, no, NO. "Prince. We are going home. And you are coming with us. End of story." I open my arms. "Come. Here."

Prince hesitates. Then he wags his tail, barks, and jumps right into my arms.

"Good boy," I say as he licks my face.

Jonah stands up and takes my hand. Together the three of us step down and through the portal.

## chapter seventeen

## Hello Again

We land right on the basement floor. I'm still holding Prince.

"You are almost ready," a soft female voice says.

What? I look around the room. "Who said that?" I ask.

"Maryrose did!" Jonah squeals.

"Seriously?" I ask.

"Seriously!"

"But what are we almost ready for?" I ask, turning to look at the mirror. "What does that mean?"

I hear stomping overhead. Lots of stomping. Parental stomping.

"Crumbs," I say, scared.

*"Ruff, ruff, ruff!"* Prince barks.

"How long have we been gone?" Jonah asks.

"I don't know! I traded my watch! What if we were gone for days?"

"They might think we ran away! Or were kidnapped!"

We run upstairs and find both our parents in the kitchen.

It's pitch-black outside. The clock on the microwave says it's 12:35 A.M. Wait. Does that mean we were only gone for thirty-five minutes? Maybe the watch wasn't broken after all?

Why are my parents up?

My mother is on the phone. Her jaw drops when she sees us. "They're here! They're here!" she yells into the phone.

My father rushes over and envelops us in a tight hug.

"Where were you?" my mother roars. "It's the middle of the night! I called the police!"

The police? She turns her back on us. "Officer . . . I just found them. I'm sorry for troubling you. . . . Oh, they will have a lot of explaining to do."

She hangs up the phone just as Dad finishes hugging us. Mom hugs us, too, but her face is stormy. "Where *were* you?" she demands. "We looked everywhere!"

"We were in the basement," I mumble.

My mom narrows her eyes. "We looked in the basement. You weren't there."

"Why in the world were you in the basement at midnight?" my dad asks. "And why are your clothes muddy?"

"We were . . ." I look at Jonah for help.

"Playing hide-and-seek!" he finishes. "It's really dirty behind the furniture."

"You were playing hide-and-seek at midnight?" my mom asks.

"Why were you awake?" Jonah asks my parents, which maybe isn't the best question right now.

"We heard Prince barking," my dad says. "I thought he was stuck downstairs, so I went to check on him. But he wasn't there. And then I checked on both of you in your rooms, and you weren't there. . . ." His voice trails off. "We thought something had happened to you."

"We were terrified," my mom adds, her lower lip trembling.

"I'm so sorry," I say, meaning it. I can only imagine how afraid my parents were. I can't believe I was responsible for it. I never want them to feel so terrified again.

Does that mean I can never go through the mirror again? Hmm. No. Next time, I'll just be more careful.

"You're both in a lot of trouble," my dad says sternly.

Jonah picks up Prince and buries his face in the dog's fur. "You're not going to take away Prince, are you?"

"No," my dad says, "he's part of the family now. But maybe no TV. Or playdates. Or rock climbing . . ."

"We'll think about it," my mom says. "But *definitely* no more hide-and-seek in the middle of the night. No more going into the basement at all in the middle of the night. Promise?"

My heart sinks. I steal a glance at Jonah. He's waiting to see what I say.

I have no choice. I can't cause my parents so much worry. I have to make the promise.

"I promise," I say, instantly feeling sad.

Good-bye, Maryrose.

Good-bye, fairy tales.

Jonah follows my lead. "I promise, too," he says softly.

"Now go back to your beds immediately," my dad orders.

"Sorry, Mom," I say, looking at the floor. "Sorry, Dad."

"Yeah," Jonah says. "We didn't mean to worry you."

"We'll talk about it more in the morning," my dad says. "Go to bed."

"Do you smell onion?" I hear my mom ask my dad as Jonah and I drag ourselves upstairs, Prince at our heels.

I feel terrible as I wave good night to Jonah and Prince and disappear inside my room. I glance at my jewelry box. There are still so many fairy tales to visit. There's *Aladdin* and *Beauty and the Beast* and *The Snow Queen* and even *Hansel and Gretel.* . . .

Oh! Look at that! I see Rapunzel! The *new* Rapunzel! Her hair is long again. Not as long as it used to be, but down to her shoulders. She looks like she's standing on a stage, and her mouth is open. Like she's singing! And in the background, I see three other people on the stage. One of them is definitely Prince Tristan. But who are the other two? One is a woman and one is a man. Both look a little older than my parents. The woman is playing the drums. And the drums say PICKLES, RAPUNZEL, AND PARENTS. Oh! They're Rapunzel's parents! Rapunzel must have found them! And now they're all in a band together!

I study Rapunzel. She's smiling as she sings. She looks happy. Even with her new hairstyle. She'd thought that her *loooong* hair was what made her unique. That her hair was what made her special.

But she's more than just her hair. And maybe she's even better off without her hair. She didn't have to suffer for years, and she still ended up with her prince. Plus, she found her parents *and* a singing career. So maybe sometimes the thing you think you need — the thing you think makes you special — isn't really that important.

Like being a spelling bee champion.

I reach into my backpack and take out the certificate Ms. Masserman gave me. It reads **THIS IS TO CERTIFY THAT ABBY PARTICIPATED IN OUR CLASS SPELLING BEE.** Thinking of Rapunzel, I hang the certificate up on my bulletin board.

I *still* want to be spelling bee champion. And maybe next year, or the year after that, I will be. Or maybe not.

But maybe that's okay. Because I'm more than just the girl who came in ninth in the spelling bee. I'm a big sister. I'm a good friend. I'm a future judge.

I'm a spelling bee participant.

I look back at my jewelry box. I'm also a fairy tale lover. And a fairy tale traveler.

At least — I was a fairy tale traveler. Not anymore.

I sigh as I change into my pajamas. I can't help wondering: Is Rapunzel better off having met us? Am I better off having gone through the mirror?

I glance at the image of Rapunzel's new band. And then back up at my new certificate.

Probably. And yes. Definitely, yes.

But if we're both better off, then how can I stop going through the mirror? I can't. I shouldn't. I shake my head. I *have* to stop. I promised I would stop.

I don't want to stop.

I turn my lights off, get into bed, and pull my covers over my chin.

What if I told my parents the mirror's secret? Would they believe it? Would they try to get rid of the mirror so we wouldn't go through? Would they want to go through with us?

So many questions.

I glance once more at my jewelry box before closing my eyes.

So many possibilities.

# acknowledgments

Thank you to . . .

The publishing folks: Laura Dail, Tamar Rydzinski, Deb Shapiro, Brian Lipson, Aimee Friedman, Abby McAden, David Levithan, Becky Amsel, Tracy van Straaten, Jennifer Ung, Bess Braswell, Whitney Steller, Sue Flynn, Rachael Hicks, Lizette Serrano, Emily Sharpe, Emily Heddleson, Becky Shapiro, Candace Greene, and AnnMarie Anderson.

The friends, writers and others: Emily Jenkins (thank you, thank you, thank you for the great notes), Courtney Sheinmel, Anne Heltzel, Lauren Myracle, Emily Bender, Tori, Carly and Carol Adams, Targia Alphonse, Jess Braun, Lauren Kisilevsky, Bonnie Altro, Corinne and Michael Bilerman, Jess Rothenberg, Jen E. Smith, Robin Wasserman, Adele Griffin, Milan Popelka, Leslie Margolis, Maryrose Wood, Tara Altebrando, Sara Zarr, Ally Carter, Jennifer Barnes, Alan Gratz, Penny Fransblow, Maggie Marr, Farrin Jacobs, and Peter Glassman.

The family: Aviva, Dad, Louisa, Robert, Gary, Lori, Sloane, Isaac, Vickie, John, Gary, Darren, Ryan, Jack, Jen, Teri, Briana,

Michael, David, Patsy, Murray, Maggie, and Jenny. Special thanks to my mom, Elissa Ambrose, for all her lightning-speed editorial help!

Extra thanks and extra love to my husband, Todd, and our daughters, Anabelle and Chloe. I love you three SO SO SO much.

The readers: You guys are the best.

And finally: I wish you all a lifetime of great hair days.

**READ ON FOR A SNEAK PEEK AT ABBY
AND JONAH'S NEXT ADVENTURE!**

# Whatever After #6

## COLD AS ICE

Suddenly, a woman — well, more like a teenager — rises onto the roof beside Prince. Her hair is silver, long, and curly, her eyes are ice blue, and she's wearing a long white dress and a white fur cloak. Her skin sparkles like it's covered in body glitter.

My breath catches in my throat.

She's the Snow Queen. She has to be. I can't take my eyes off her. Even though she's the queen of cold, she's as mesmerizing as fire.

"Stop making such a racket, you mutt," she says to Prince, her voice as cold as ice.

Her words send a pulse of fear through my entire body. Jonah slinks behind me.

"Is that Elsa?" Jonah asks.

"That is *not* Elsa," I say softly. This snow queen is terrifying. "Where did she come from?" I wonder out loud. "Did she just magically appear?" Kai pops up onto the roof next, holding the sticks in his hand. He inserts them into the snowman that was missing arms. "Did he just appear, too?" I ask.

"No, they both came up a staircase in the middle of the roof. It's behind Prince."

Aha.

*Ruff, ruff, ruff, ruff!* Prince calls to us. He's jumping up and down. Exactly like he does when we get home from school. His whole body is trembling with excitement.

"Stop that yapping immediately," the Snow Queen tells him, "or you'll regret it."

"Oh, no," I murmur. It feels like the moment before a storm. The air gets heavy and dark. Something awful is about to happen, I know it.

Jonah is trying to motion with his hands for Prince to be quiet, but instead of listening, our puppy just wags his tail harder and barks even louder.

The Snow Queen steps closer to Prince. "Don't say I didn't warn you," she says. Then she leans toward him and puckers her lips. What is she doing?

"Prince!" I yell. "Run, Prince, run!"

With her lips all rounded, the Snow Queen looks like she's blowing Prince a kiss. But it's not a kiss. I can actually see the air that comes out of her mouth. It's like steam from a kettle. A tiny white tornado.

Prince lifts his paws and starts to run.

The kiss hits him, and he slows down, looking dazed. The

Snow Queen puckers up again and another tornado shoots out of her mouth.

"I'm scared," Jonah says, his voice trembling.

"Prince!" I yell again.

A sad sound escapes Prince's doggie mouth and then he freezes in mid-motion. He solidifies in place. One paw up about to take a step, his tail still on high alert. His fur gets a white glaze all over. He looks like a dog who's been locked in a freezer for too long. He looks like he has freezer burn. He looks —

I gasp. I feel a stab in my heart.

He looks frozen.

The Snow Queen just froze my dog.

**Each time Abby and Jonah get sucked into their magic mirror, they wind up in a different fairy tale — and find new adventures!**

**Read all the**
**Whatever After books!**

**www.scholastic.com/whateverafter**